Dukes Prefer Bluestockings

CHARLOTTE BUTTERWORTH may be on her first London season, but she already knows she will never marry. Nothing interests her as much as numbers, and numbers seem to be of absolutely no interest to anyone else. And then there's...the secret.

Callum Montgomery, Duke of Vernon, can marry the best. He's handsome and charming and perfect. In fact, he's been betrothed to the darling of the ton since he was seven, even if he does keep on putting off the wedding.

When the roguish Duke of Vernon gains possession of some terrible, utterly shocking news about Charlotte, Charlotte needs to act quickly to keep the duke from revealing her secret.

Other books in the *Wedding Trouble* series:

Don't Tie the Knot

The Earl's Christmas Consultant

How to Train a Viscount

A Kiss for the Marquess

A Holiday Proposal

Prologue

SCOTLAND

1798

Callum Montgomery, Duke of Vernon, had not always possessed a habit of perching on Lord McIntyre's roof, but everything had changed since the *incident*.

Before the incident, Callum had still been able to sleep.

Before the incident, Callum's parents had been alive. Callum might be only seven, but he knew parents should be alive. They were supposed to wave him off when he went to Eton for the first time, and his father was supposed to teach him cards.

Before the incident, Callum had lived in a castle with steep roofs. Lord McIntyre's manor home was flat. Callum's twin brother Hamish said that made the manor home less artistic, but Callum thought it made the roof better for climbing, even though the earl shouted at him whenever he caught him. Lord McIntyre said he cared about Callum's health, but the earl's interest did not extend to anything other than that Callum should remain alive.

Snowflakes fell, even though their shapes were not visible in the dark night, and Callum shivered. *No matter.* Outside was still the nicest place to be, even if the icy breeze shaped the waves below into tall, violent forms. Lord McIntyre was unlikely to spot him here. Most likely, his guardian was sleeping. Even Hamish slept.

Callum crept along the roof, crunching over the occasional slab of snow. Stars glowed above him, and in the distance he could see the outline of Montgomery Castle.

Lord McIntyre had told Callum that one day when he was older he might live in the castle again, but that Callum's parents had been very bad and had spent all their money. He said it made sense that his parents had been bad, because Callum was a very naughty boy. He said Callum should be grateful he'd taken over Callum's parents' mortgage, and that one day, if Callum married his daughter Isla, Callum would be able to live in the castle again. Callum didn't understand why the earl wanted his daughter to marry someone he hated, but adults could be strange.

A vague noise sounded in the distance, growing louder and more recognizable over the waves.

A carriage.

Callum wrinkled his brow. *It can't be. Carriages don't normally drive here.* The closest town was miles away, and this was winter. Patches of ice and snow still covered some parts of the roads. The cliffs were steep, and the servants said if a carriage ran off the road anyone inside would die.

And yet the sound of wheels grinding over gravel and of horses trotting seemed distinctly carriage-like.

Callum inched toward the edge of his perch and held onto one of the scary looking gables. The gable was decorated with tiny steps, even though the steps didn't lead anywhere. Hamish said the steps didn't need to lead anywhere to be pretty, but Callum thought decorating windows with steps was confusing.

The carriage looked more elegant than the ones servants traveled in. Servants traveled in black carriages, but this one had cheerful yellow wheels.

The horses stopped, and the great door opened. Someone hurried over the gravel and snow to greet the visitor. A lavender coat flashed in lantern light, and Callum drew back. Normally the butler greeted visitors, but no butler wore lavender and so much lace. Callum knew. He liked observing the household.

It's the earl.

Lord McIntyre glanced around, and Callum drew in his breath quickly and pressed his body against the edge of the gable.

The earl opened the carriage door, and a lady stepped out. She wore a long dark coat trimmed with fur. Isla would have loved her coat, but Callum's attention was drawn to her blond hair.

Aunt Edwina?

Other women were also slender, and other women also wore nice attire.

Lord McIntyre always said selecting clothes was the only thing which women were good at.

Callum stilled, keeping his gaze on the woman. His heartbeat quickened, like musicians had taken hold of it and were drumming a celebratory tune, even though Callum was still unsure whether there was anything to celebrate.

The woman strode closer to the earl and stepped into the glow of the man's lantern. The faint light flashed over the woman's face, shaped like a heart, shaped exactly like Aunt Edwina's.

His heartbeat continued to quicken, and this time, he knew her appearance was only something to celebrate.

My aunt.

My only relative besides Hamish.

He hadn't seen her since before the *incident.* Lord McIntyre had told him she was angry at him, and that only Lord McIntyre cared about him, even though Lord McIntyre frequently scolded him.

"Good evening." The earl lowered his torso in an appropriate manner at odds with his icy tone.

"My lord." She curtsied, though less deeply than the servants. Perhaps she was wary of putting her dress too deeply into the snow. "I'm sorry to come at this hour."

"You should be," Lord McIntyre grumbled.

"I wasn't expecting to see you."

"It's my manor house."

"Indeed," she said smoothly, and turned her head, as if half-expecting to see some servants.

Servants always greeted Callum when he arrived in a carriage. They should greet Aunt Edwina. She was an adult, and she'd been the sister-in-law of a duke. Even though he was a duke, and his friend Wolfe was a viscount and would be an earl one day, everyone else seemed to think their ranks most impressive and unusual.

Callum slid farther down the roof. Perhaps he should announce his presence to Aunt Edwina. But might she worry? Adults seemed to worry whenever he was up a tree. Adults didn't seem very brave, even though they were the ones who went to war.

One day Callum would go to war, and he wouldn't be scared.

"Your letter surprised me," Lord McIntyre said.

"It shouldn't have," Aunt Edwina retorted.

"I assure you of my capabilities in looking after your nephews," Lord McIntyre said, retaining that same silky tone which Callum had grown to despise.

"That will not be necessary, my lord," Aunt Edwina said.

Joy sprang through Callum's heart. Was it possible he would not need to stay with Lord and Lady McIntyre? He liked playing with Wolfe and Isla, but he didn't want to live with them forever.

"How are my nephews?"

"Their limbs are all intact, and they have not succumbed to any fever. The young duke's temperament, however—" Lord McIntyre broke off, as if he could not bear to utter Callum's instances of disobedience.

Callum's cheeks heated, despite the consistent fall of snowflakes.

I'm not bad. I'm not bad. I'm not bad.

"I would like to see them," Aunt Edwina said.

Lord McIntyre hesitated. "You can see them in the morning."

"Very well," Aunt Edwina said. "They will soon be living with me."

"In Edinburgh? With no husband?" Lord McIntyre laughed, but it sounded forced.

Joviality was not a characteristic Callum associated with the earl.

"Foolish woman," Lord McIntyre said. "What sort of life is that for them? They're two rowdy boys. Cities are dangerous places."

"Then I'll move here." Aunt Edwina lifted her chin. "To Montgomery Castle."

Excitement coursed through Callum. Maybe they could go back. They could live like *before.* It wouldn't be the same, but he'd always liked his aunt.

"Balderdash. You have no claim on the castle," Lord McIntyre said.

"More than you," Aunt Edwina retorted. "Besides, I don't require a claim. Callum is the duke."

"My dear, Miss Lacey," Lord McIntyre said. "I am afraid that you do not know all the details. The complexity of the law is rather beyond you."

"I doubt that," Aunt Edwina said in an equally icy manner.

The tone seemed to work, for Lord McIntyre stiffened. "Please come inside. We can discuss things in the morning."

"I suppose that will do," Aunt Edwina said.

"Good, good," Lord McIntyre said.

Callum had never heard Lord McIntyre sound so nice before. Perhaps he was grateful he would no longer need to look after Callum. Perhaps the man was relieved.

Callum leaned over the roof. Possibly Hamish would be able to contain his excitement, but not Callum. He had to greet her. She wanted to see him. "Aunt Edwina! I'm here."

Lord McIntyre and Aunt Edwina tilted their heads.

"What on earth are you doing there?" Lord McIntyre said.

Normally his guardian might have shouted, but maybe because it was late and he didn't want to wake anyone up, or maybe because he was happy Callum's aunt was going to take him away, he maintained a low volume.

"I heard the carriage," Callum lied. Lord McIntyre was not required to know that Callum had developed a passion for illicit roof perching.

"Darling boy." Aunt Edwina beamed. "How nice to see you. You're going to live with me. Just how it's supposed to be."

Callum had heard her tell that to Lord McIntyre, but hearing her tell him directly caused energy to surge through him. He grinned and clapped his hands.

"Don't topple down," Lord McIntyre said hastily. "Go to bed."

"We'll speak tomorrow," Aunt Edwina promised.

"I'm so happy." Callum beamed and then walked easily over the roof and opened the window. He glanced at Hamish, but his brother still slept. There would be plenty of time to tell him about Aunt Edwina's arrival in the morning. They'd see her soon.

The next morning, Callum ran downstairs with excitement he could scarcely contain. Aunt Edwina would be there.

But only Lady McIntyre occupied the dining room, and she knew nothing about Aunt Edwina's arrival. Lord McIntyre wasn't present, and so Callum went to eat in the nursery with Wolfe and Isla.

Aunt Edwina still wasn't there when he finished breakfast.

"The servants didn't mention her arrival," Lady McIntyre said after he asked her, "but it's possible she's sleeping."

Oh.

That made sense.

"She arrived late," Callum said.

Lady McIntyre gave him a patient smile, the same smile, he realized, that she gave when Isla made up stories of being a princess and having fought dragons herself. *Never mind.* She would see soon. They all would. Callum was going to return to Montgomery Castle with Hamish, and they would never need to live with their neighbors again.

But when Aunt Edwina didn't appear for the evening meal, Callum knew something was wrong. No one slept that long.

He grabbed his wooden sword and marched through all the rooms, even though Lord McIntyre had told him he should remain in the nursery.

She wasn't in the nicest bedroom with the blue curtains, and she wasn't in the smallest bedroom that had no curtains.

His heart beat loudly, as if it were a drum and he were really at war and carrying a real sword.

The earl will know.

Lord McIntyre hadn't been here earlier, which was strange, but maybe he would be here now.

Callum stopped before Lord McIntyre's study.

Lord McIntyre's study was the scariest place in the manor house. It smelled of cigar smoke, and all the furniture was old and heavy and dark. Hamish said the furniture was medieval and that it was very special, but Callum knew the only way it was special was at being scary.

Lord McIntyre was at his desk when Callum opened the door, and Callum firmed his grip on his sword.

Lord McIntyre lifted his quizzing glass and peered at Callum. He placed it down abruptly. "Of course it's you. Your brother has too much sense to disturb a busy man."

"You'd rather Hamish were the duke," Callum said.

Lord McIntyre shrugged. "He's more suited to the role."

Heat soared up Callum's face.

"I've yet to see your brother come barging into my office carrying a toy sword," Lord McIntyre continued and he steepled his fingers. "He's a child of far more propriety. You would do well to observe him."

Callum's knuckles tightened around his wooden sword. "Where is Aunt Edwina?"

The man's gaze moved to the side, and he tapped his fingers against a glass of caramel colored liquid. "Your aunt? Oh, dear me. Why would you ask me about her?"

"Because she was here. Last night."

"That's impossible." The man's face remained placid, devoid of any emotion, though his gaze darted again to his side.

"You spoke with her. *I* spoke to her." Callum's voice shook.

Why doesn't he remember?

Callum knew adults sometimes forgot things. His grandfather had always been forgetting things before he died, but somehow he hadn't expected it of the earl.

"Perhaps you had a dream," Lord McIntyre said gently, even though gentle was hardly a common occurrence.

"I-I didn't." Callum despised his stammer. He jutted his chin out and widened his shoulders, like the poses his tin soldiers had. Unlike one of the soldier's enemies, the earl didn't look frightened.

"Dreams are natural." Lord McIntyre maintained a soothing tone, as if he were reading a bedtime story, even though the earl never read to them. He didn't even read to Wolfe or Isla. The earl tapped his fingers together. "I suppose if you were very young and very unfamiliar with the world, you *might* confuse them with reality. Naturally, *my* children would never do that. Wolfe and Isla, and yes, even Hamish, are far too clever. But you... I could see *you* being confused."

Callum stiffened. It hadn't been a dream. He remembered the sound of the carriage, the appearance of his aunt, the discussion with Lord McIntyre.

"I'm not a baby," Callum mumbled.

"I should hope not." Lord McIntyre exhaled and discomfort seemed to flicker over him. "Still, since you are here now, I may as well tell you something. I am afraid it is bad news."

"Oh?" Callum shifted his legs. He wanted to run and tell Hamish that Lord McIntyre was lying, and that he was unworthy of Hamish's admiration.

"It concerns your Aunt Edwina." Lord McIntyre gestured to a seat. "Please, have a seat."

Callum swallowed hard and approached the tall wooden chair. He'd never sat in it before. He climbed onto it and slid himself back. The carvings dug into his clothes, but he returned his gaze to the earl.

"I am afraid your aunt is dead," Lord McIntyre said abruptly.

Callum blinked. "She can't be. I just saw her—"

"You had a dream," Lord McIntyre said sternly.

Callum was silent. Had he dreamed about her?

"She died near here," the earl said. "She was evidently making her way to this manor house when her carriage fell over the cliff."

"Impossible," Callum said.

But she wasn't here.

He'd checked all the bedrooms.

Lord McIntyre was the only other person who'd seen her, and he was lying.

Why was he lying? Unless...

"You murdered her!" Callum shouted.

Lord McIntyre looked away. "Balderdash."

"I don't know how, but you must have."

"Let me be clear," Lord McIntyre said. "I am an earl and a valued member of the community. You are a boy."

"I know things," Callum said.

"Would you like me to tell your brother about the truth about your parents' deaths?" Lord McIntyre asked.

"What do you mean?" Callum asked softly.

"About how you caused them to die?" Lord McIntyre continued, smiling.

"I-I didn't," Callum said, shifting in his seat.

"Your mother told you not to play with the village children," Lord McIntyre said. "But you didn't listen, did you? You were naughty."

Callum swallowed hard.

"And then you got sick."

"I'm fine now," Callum insisted.

"But you made your parents sick. And they died."

"That wasn't because of me," Callum said softly, but he wasn't certain.

Had he made them sick? Was it because of him?

Lord McIntyre cleaned his quizzing glass and placed it back on. Light shone on the glass, and the earl's face appeared distorted. "If you had only listened to them, they would still be here."

Callum's heart didn't drum any sort of tune. It hardly drummed at all. The world got too hot, as if it had decided to thrust Callum into the hellfire some of the servants whispered about. Callum forced himself to take a breath, forced himself to direct his gaze at the earl. "I-I didn't know."

"Now whom do you think people will believe?" Lord McIntyre mused. "A respected earl, given to bettering the lives of others to such an extent he's taken in the impoverished sons of his neighbors after their most tragic deaths? Or you—a seven-year-old boy who always misbehaves?"

Normally Callum might have clenched his fists, but the action seemed too demanding. His fingers felt numb, and even breathing seemed to have entered an athletic category. And unlike cricket, a sport Callum enjoyed, simple inhalation and exhalation seemed almost impossible.

"Do you think Hamish would like to hear about how you are the reason your parents died?"

Callum shrank back into the uncomfortable chair. "N-no."

He despised how small he felt.

I didn't mean to kill them.

Lord McIntyre smirked, like a hunter already imagining the taste of his prey. "Then you will be silent."

Callum flinched. He wanted to tell Hamish. He wanted to tell Lady McIntyre. Instead, they would just think he'd imagined his aunt's presence.

But Hamish was his twin brother, and now Callum's only relative in the world. How could Callum tell him he was behind their parents' deaths? Hamish was always telling Callum to behave, and now he would know the extent of Callum's horribleness.

Callum stiffened. *But Lord McIntyre killed Aunt Edwina on purpose.* He hadn't killed his parents on purpose. He hadn't known they would get sick and die if he played with the other children.

He wanted everyone to know Lord McIntyre was terrible.

But Lord McIntyre was right. He was just a boy. What could he do?

One day I will be an adult.

One day I'll get revenge.

Chapter One

APRIL, 1816

The trouble with London in the spring was the profusion of weddings.

The buildings remained as majestic as in other seasons, but people thronged the streets. Children and people who should have been sufficiently old to resist sentimental notions on marriage scattered petals with glee over the tilestones, even though any observer could see they didn't know the couple.

Charlotte Butterworth directed the horses to move briskly past St. George's, and the cart ground over fallen petals. Blossoms swathed the trees in pink and ivory and a thick floral scent Parisian *parfumeurs* no doubt strove to imitate filled the air. It was the sort of spring day which sent artists into a flurry of activity, and she passed more than one furrowed brow as someone peered over an easel. Some people might laud the compilation of colorful petals on the ground, but Charlotte had always found it an improvement when petals were attached to flowers. The petals that flitted through the air and landed on her dress, gloves, and bonnet with no discrimination, were certainly not an improvement, and she attempted to sweep them away while holding the reins.

I'm going to be late.

Charlotte had worked out the precise time it took to go from her parents' home to Dr. Hutton's office, but she had failed to take into the account that this was prime wedding season.

Normally, Charlotte never made mistakes. Normally, though, she didn't receive stern letters from physicians demanding her presence. Still, at least her miscalculation could be explained by the fact she always took her daily ride in the afternoon, when any engaged couples were safely wed, sated from their wedding breakfast, if nervous about everything else.

One day it might be you.

Charlotte pushed away the thought. Bluestockings were objects of jokes rather than marriage proposals. Her sister Georgiana was already on her third season, with not even the most tenuous of prospects, and mama had always said it would be easier to marry Georgiana off than Charlotte. A passion for gardens was easier to explain than a passion for numbers.

She entered Grosvenor Square, averting her eyes lest any of the *ton* recognize her. Her family's groom might be sitting at the back of the cart, but he would be deemed an imperfect chaperone. She might be considered socially inept, but she knew no one could discover her destination.

My family has enough to worry about.

Besides, though crime in London might be high, Grosvenor Street was no cesspool of infamy. Charlotte was prone to driving by herself in Norfolk, and by the time she returned, her family would only be just rising.

She lifted her chin and urged the horses forward, ignoring the occasional upward eyebrow from someone accustomed to the unwritten rules of high society being followed. She brushed aside the twinge of guilt that she'd assured her family's maid she was only going to call on a friend.

It will be nothing, Charlotte assured herself. *Absolutely nothing.*

At last, she entered Hyde Park. She did not linger, no matter how pleasing the view of trees reflecting over the Serpentine or how spectacular the shades of blossoms were. No doubt she'd have the opportunity to see artistic renditions of the scenery later, proudly displayed by some matchmaking mama as testament to her son's sensitive nature, as if a habit of dabbing brushes with watercolors could make people overlook dilapidating estates and coffers emptied at the nearest gaming hell.

Unfortunately, Rotten Row was not devoid of people. The bright sunshine had evidently inspired some members of the *ton* to personally exercise their horses. They veered their heads toward each collection of flowers with regularity. Women had selected sumptuous gowns, adorned with flounces and netting, for the occasion. They seemed unconcerned that neither flounces nor netting were conducive to outside enjoyment, and Charlotte felt self-conscious in her sensible gray muslin dress.

The sunbeams remained pleasantly warm, and the birds chirped spontaneous symphonies. *Everything will be fine.* The office's letter had been stern, but that merely meant the writer might be well-suited to be an exasperated governess or tutor.

Nothing more.

Her chest still squeezed, and she pressed the horses to hasten.

CALLUM ATTEMPTED TO ignore the pain in his head and drew the curtains shut. The velvet fabric was an inadequate barrier to the sounds of festivity. Hades' Lair could normally be counted on to be a luxurious retreat, but today laughter penetrated even that fortress of disrepute.

"I despise weddings," Callum grumbled.

Wolfe snorted and lifted his gaze from a letter. "I believe you've expressed that opinion before. I take it you don't want to marry my sister at St. George's?"

Damnation.

When Callum had agreed to marry his guardian's daughter, he'd been seven. Marriage had been an abstract concept, but now it was rather less so.

The new Earl of McIntyre might be his best friend, a bond most people would classify as the close variety, but they'd known one day they would be closer. One day they would be true brothers.

He sighed. He remembered his childhood vow to seek revenge on Wolfe's father. His guardian had died during the war.

"It's too early to consider a venue." Callum forced himself to laugh.

"You've waited long enough." An icy tone flitted through Wolfe's voice. It was a tone with which Callum was familiar. Wolfe's father, the late Lord McIntyre, had used it often. Callum had never expected Wolfe to direct it at him, and a chill crept up his spine.

"The war is over," Wolfe said, as if Callum could ever have forgotten he no longer needed to dodge sword slashes and cannonballs. "Celebrate. Be merry. Be *married.*"

"Of course. One day." Callum gave Wolfe one of the charming smiles for which he was known. Unfortunately, perhaps because Wolfe was male, or perhaps because Wolfe had known Callum all his life, the man was unmoved.

"See that it's by the end of the summer," Wolfe said, and even though his friend's eyes had a habit of habit of sparkling, they appeared stern. "Isla is not getting younger. You can live in that great big castle of yours in the Highlands. You'll love it."

"Aye." Callum nodded his head with a vigor he hoped Wolfe couldn't feel was feigned.

Callum knew Wolfe was right. Isla was his destiny, and he shouldn't be dawdling about St. Peter's gates, when everlasting happiness lay nearby.

It was just—

His chest tightened.

He didn't love her.

"Don't worry about the debt. My father always intended to void your parents' debts once you married Isla," Wolfe said airily, but if he intended to convey generosity, Callum only heard a threat. "We'll be family."

Callum didn't want to nod.

Everyone had been talking about his nuptials to Lady Isla practically once he'd stopped barreling about in padded pudding caps, constrained by his leading strings. They'd lauded the good fortune they'd been born in the same year and remarked on how lovely Lady Isla's dark hair would appear besides Callum's fairer strands. Duty, they told him, would never be so pleasant.

And indeed, Lady Isla met any criterion for excellence. She was beautiful in the same way her brother Wolfe was handsome. Her features were strong: a straight nose, wide-set eyes, and an athletic figure formed from years of running over the Highlands. She was everything he should desire, and yet... He hadn't chosen her.

Callum's stomach soured. The fact was likely explained by the quantity and variety of drink they'd indulged in. *Nothing else.*

"Wolfe?" A voice sounded outside. The pitch might be low and melodic, the sort of alto other men might easily describe in exuberant terms, but it sent a rush of worry through Callum.

Isla.

She was here, in this dashed gaming hell. He supposed her presence here might be made respectable because her brother was one of the proprietors and because she was not searching for a husband.

The temperature of the room surged, and Callum rubbed sweat from the back of his neck, conscious that his hand shook, as if the action were novel. He darted his gaze at the door. "I-I have an appointment."

"Nonsense," Wolfe said.

Callum rose and backed toward the door. Perhaps the voice belonged to a different woman. More than one madam had barged into the gaming hell, armed with business plans, a proposition Wolfe and he had always refused.

But if he were wrong...

I'm being foolish.

But his legs still swayed. He remembered that blasted meeting with his former guardian all those years ago. He remembered his conviction the old earl had murdered his aunt.

Now he wasn't certain.

Had he imagined her presence after all?

And yet marrying Lady Isla, making all his late guardian's dreams come true, seemed suddenly impossible.

Perhaps he could investigate the matter.

Callum and Wolfe might have played cricket as seven-year olds, but everything had changed from the time when the crown of achievement had been praise from the nearest gardener.

Callum had been able to avoid pondering Aunt Edwina's death.

The war had occupied his attention. The blood might have washed away from the flat plains of France and Belgium, the soldiers who had given their cries of agony might have long been buried, and Callum and his regiment might have returned to British soil, confident they'd saved the world from a belligerent border expander, but now the faint memories of his life before the war haunted him.

The returned officers and he frequented the same clubs and the same gaming hells, trying not to dwell on the fact the last time they'd worked together it had mattered, but now nothing they did mattered.

They had good memories, of course, but even those memories were important to forget, to not dwell on the fact that the most worthy thing one had done in one's life was killing former members in Bonaparte's *Grand Armee de Paysans*, one's worth to the army determined by one's ability to lead one's troops to take lives with a similar, merciless ease.

No. Callum had found it easier to drink and feel the burn of whisky tumble down his throat. Whatever Wolfe's faults, and his father was chief among them, Wolfe was diverting. Callum had known that the old earl would have abhorred his son running a gaming hell, and Callum had been happy to assist. Better that than to recall the pummel of a bullet through one's skin, pondering whether one's body could resist an overwhelming compulsion to faint, despite the pain and ever-increasing sense of lightheadedness, so one could continue to live, continue to kill, continue to fight for Britain.

But now things had changed.

Wolfe desired him to make good on his engagement to his sister.

Callum needed to think.

He couldn't wildly accuse Wolfe's father of murder.

Perhaps he should marry her. Wolfe was his best friend after all, and Lady Isla was decent.

And yet—

I need time.

Callum hurried out the door.

"Wait," Wolfe shouted, but Callum didn't want to wait. He didn't even look behind him. Instead, he rushed through the corridor, wishing the club had been somewhat less successful, so the corridor would lack the multitude of sharp-edged furniture.

Finally, he pushed through the heavy wooden doors and stepped into the corridor. Fragrant scents invaded his nostrils, as if to distract him from the seriousness of Isla's presence. She'd been safely away in Scotland, but now she was here, everything had changed.

Callum sent a longing glance at his curricle. He was almost tempted to grab some horses from the stable and hitch them up himself. Still, that would take time, and time was not something he possessed.

He dashed through the streets. People could stare; it didn't matter. Dukes were allowed eccentricities. It wouldn't do anything to hamper people's interest in thrusting their daughters at him, and so far even running a gaming hell hadn't compelled the proprietresses of Almack's to refuse entry into that most lofty and lackluster establishment.

He sprinted toward the park, until his footsteps finally pounded on dirt rather than cobblestones and a floral scent invaded his nostrils.

"Vernon!" Wolfe's voice was unmistakable and barreled toward him, even though the earl was supposed to be in Hades' Lair, perhaps flummoxing his servants with requests for tea with which to entertain his sister.

Callum darted his gaze about Hyde Park. If only he'd run toward the city after all. Parks had a dearth of hiding spots. Flowers might be pretty, but their tendency toward compactness was not conducive to hiding. The trunks of the trees were similarly imperfect. Callum was no scrawny dandy. Muscles like his had a habit of being visible, a fact made evident by the number of debutantes and married women who fawned over him, even when they were not yet aware of his title and its accompanying significance.

Muscles were entirely without use now. There was no steed on which to jump, and certainly no roof upon which to clamber, in a manner more familiar in adventure stories written by the like of Loretta van Lochen. There was only grass, flowers, trees and—

Trees.

Perhaps he might not be successful in hiding behind a tree, but he could certainly *climb* one. He dashed away from the path, and then scrambled up a tree, thankful for the expertise in tree climbing he'd gained in Scotland. His brother Hamish had strived to conform to Lord and Lady McIntyre's expectations, but even Hamish hadn't been able to resist the joys of scaling the chestnut trees that lined the estate.

Callum pulled himself onto a bough. His legs still dangled, and he crawled further along the bark surface and found a less discernible perch.

Yes.

This worked.

Wolfe still sprinted toward him, but his gaze was darting about the park and not up toward tree limbs.

Good.

Callum relaxed against the familiar rough texture of the branches. The blossoms were rather less familiar. Spring days had a tendency to shower, and Callum struggled to remember if he'd ever climbed a tree when it had been in full bloom.

Though a tree covered with blossoms should be as convenient as a tree covered in leaves, the tiny pink and white buds, no matter how often their beauty was extolled, irritated his eyes. They fluttered about, drifting down around him.

Leaves never did this. Leaves were far superior.

Callum shifted his position on the branch, but no place was secure from the consistent flutter of white and pink petals. His nose twitched.

Blast.

Callum was the Duke of Vernon. He came from a good Scottish family. He wasn't going to succumb to a sneeze. That was the sort of thing that might have him lose his balance and lead to immediate discovery. Callum had attended the theater. He knew how these things happened.

His nose twitched again, and his eyes stung. The pink and white petals clung to his attire, and a bird tilted his head at him, perhaps disgruntled at the oversized company.

"Vernon!" Wolfe hollered. "You must be here somewhere."

At least Wolfe had not chosen to call him by his Christian name like some naughty boy. That seemed a meager consolation, and some of the well-dressed members of the *ton* halted their strolls in curiosity.

Callum needed to slip from this tree. He needed another way to avoid Wolfe. He needed—

Callum's gaze dropped on a cart, coming along the lane. Some chit was urging her horses forward. She'd installed her groom in the back of the cart, and Callum grinned.

Unlike Callum, this woman was *not* attired for an evening indulging in vices. Instead, she was dressed in a far more appropriate morning dress. The murky brown garment could be the definition of practical, and her fichu left everything to the imagination.

The woman had evidently decided to brave the park with no chaperone.

Well, she'd left room for him.

Jumping into a strange woman's cart was unideal, but at least he wasn't jumping into the carriage of someone he knew. One would rather get tired of apologizing. Imagine if one of the proprietresses of Almack's had been riding below. Not that a proprietress would be riding by herself.

Perhaps this was some servant, tasked to circle the park while her mistress misbehaved with some Corinthian. He glanced at the woman again. Yes, that must be it. Her attire lacked the flourish of most women of the *ton.* There was a definite dearth of flounces on her gown, and her sleeves did not possess the requisite fullness women had prided themselves in all season.

Callum inhaled and released his hold on the branch. If Wolfe saw him now, it wouldn't matter; he had an escape vehicle. He landed in the cart. Not on the ground outside the cart, a fate plummeted through the air and, with a thump, came to an abrupt halt beside the woman, pleased that he had a less accomplished person might endure. He brushed his breeches. His bottom might ache, but that was a minor matter. He turned to his new companion and grinned.

Chapter Two

THERE WAS A MAN IN Charlotte's carriage.

And not a groom or an elderly butler who'd practiced the art of being invisible. This man had broad shoulders and lanky legs and the sort of attire only made by the finest tailor and only maintained by the finest valet.

Not that the man took heed of his apparel. Leaves dotted his tailcoat, and streaks of mud stained his breeches. Most likely mud was on the other side of his breeches and was dirtying the cart.

Charlotte lurched away and squeezed against the side of the cart. She directed her gaze at him, willing him to disappear, but the man seemed distressingly solid, and she screamed.

"My turn," the stranger said smoothly, reaching for the reins. His fingers touched hers, and even through the gloves, a surge of unwelcome energy moved through her. His fingers were large, ungloved, and their position on top of hers was entirely improper.

Men's hands weren't supposed to touch women's. Charlotte might be on her first season, but she did know that, no matter how much other debutantes laughed and called her a country bumpkin. Men's hands could touch hers briefly while dancing, and they could even clasp them while kissing them during particular florid introductions, but they absolutely could not touch them otherwise.

When people said London was dangerous, Charlotte hadn't imagined men tumbling into women's carts.

Charlotte was already late. This wasn't supposed to happen. She'd planned her visit to Dr. Hutton's with care. Now this strange man was sitting beside her, sullying her cart and making her late.

"Leave," the groom demanded behind them, though Jerry's lack of muscles and squeaky voice made his statement ineffectual.

Fiddle-faddle.

Charlotte grabbed her parasol and directed the metal ferrule at the man. "It is perhaps appropriate to warn you that I intend to strike you with this."

The man's lips turned up into a decided smirk, and even his eyebrows pranced higher. His face seemed entirely composed of symmetrical planes, chiseled cheekbones and exquisite skin, the sort her sister Georgiana attempted to achieve with lemon and buttermilk masks, but never managed to obtain. Charlotte decided not to investigate his face further. It resembled those of the men at balls who never danced with her, the men with whom all the other wallflowers longed to dance, and who seemed to confine any attention toward her to the occasional smug glance.

Charlotte firmed her lips and pushed him with her parasol.

"Ow!" The man yelped and slid away, even though a cursory estimation of the cart's measurements should have allowed him to ascertain he should not have attempted to occupy it.

His knees brushed against hers, and a masculine scent of crisp cotton and lemon wafted in the air. The scent might not be precisely unpleasant, but its presence was improper. The air should smell of grass and trees and flowers, not of men.

Men weren't supposed to jump into carts.

Men weren't even supposed to speak to women they didn't know.

Charlotte forced her voice to not quiver. "I demand you leave. Your presence is undesired, and furthermore, you are causing me to be *late.*"

The man seemed unmoved. He nudged the reins and glanced behind him. Charlotte followed his gaze. Men in curricles grinned at her, as if eager to ponder something else except the speed of their conveyances. Older men and women in majestic barouches held quizzing glasses to their eyes, and even their drivers seemed to focus more on Charlotte than on Rotten Row.

Fire flared across Charlotte's cheeks, threatening to blaze with a vigor normally reserved for forest calamities. "Everyone is looking at me."

"I rather believe they're looking at *me*," the stranger said. "The important thing is, do you see a man in a green velvet waistcoat and a glossy beaver hat?"

"The one with a rather angry expression on his face? His precise distance from us is difficult to calculate given the rapid pace with which he is approaching us."

"Blast." The man scrambled up, jostling the cart further, and urged the horses to hasten. Sweat glistened over his brow, a fact that would most likely cause his valet further irritation. "Damnation."

"Cursing is an unbecoming habit," Charlotte stated, attempting some control of the conversation even as the cart veered to the left. "A dictionary is composed of a great many varied words, and I am certain with some meager deliberation even you could select a more appropriate one for this occasion."

"I am being chased." The stranger contorted his face into a scowl, though frustratingly that did not hamper the overall attractiveness of his appearance. The man was impossible.

"While being chased may be inconvenient for you, it does not require inconvenience for me. As I mentioned, and as you should have remembered, I am late for an important appointment. Timeliness is a virtue."

"I'll stop him, miss." The groom rose from his perch in the back, and the cart jostled and swerved. The groom refrained from sitting, despite the cart's current resemblance to a ship swaying under the force of an enormous ocean wave and crossed his arms. "Leave the cart at once, sir."

Charlotte grasped hold of the side of the cart, aware her lower lip was toppling to a degree unnecessary even for consuming particularly tough meats.

The groom had never said so much before.

"Sit down," the stranger said impatiently.

"I will not," the groom said valiantly.

Charlotte firmed her lips and sought to recover the reins. Unfortunately, the stranger's clutch was strong. *Well.* That fact was not surprising. The man's muscles were apparent. Butterflies decided to flutter through her chest.

The groom reached over them and yanked the reins. Evidently, he also hadn't paid sufficient attention to the stranger's muscular form, for the reins did not slip from the man's grip.

The horses neighed and launched into a gallop down a small lane, as if they were competing at Epsom and not simply pulling a cart.

The groom veered fiercely, and for a horrendous moment, Charlotte thought he might fly from the cart, but the groom hunched his back and grabbed hold of the cart's edge. "I demand you leave at once, sir."

"It's 'Your Grace,'" the stranger said.

"A d-duke?" The groom's eyes bulged, and his face paled, as if he'd transformed into a ghost. "F-forgive me, Your Grace."

"Jerry!" Charlotte exclaimed. "You mustn't apologize to him."

"He's a duke, miss." The groom's eyes remained round, and he slid down. "Practically royalty."

"That doesn't mean he's permitted to leap into people's conveyances," Charlotte said.

The groom looked uncertain. "I 'aven't met a duke before."

"Well, I assure you, they are not allowed to be devoid of manners." Charlotte decided not to mention that she'd never met a duke either.

The duke had the audacity to grin.

CALLUM WAITED FOR WONDER to fill her face. He knew the stages. He'd seen them often enough before.

Her eyes would glaze, and he would know she wasn't solely seeing him, but also the castles, town homes and estates that accompanied men with his title.

Her cheeks would flush. The excitement of being in his presence tended to surpass that of any cold weather.

Her lashes would flutter. He hadn't decided if women considered eyelash movement attractive or if they simply obtained extra energy in his presence.

She would smooth her dress, as if his presence had wrinkle-causing powers.

She would shove her locks behind her ear, as if to better hear even the smallest murmur from him, lest it be a declaration of love and an offer to make her his duchess, one which he would not be compelled to repeat at normal auditory levels.

The predictability of women was almost tiresome, and he stretched his legs as far as they would go in his cart and waited for recognition to show upon her face.

His lips twitched. Perhaps she might even faint.

The woman, though, seemed remarkably upright.

Possibly her stays were of excellent quality.

"Indeed," she said coolly. Her eyes remained resolute, and since the sky had chosen to be gray sometime last year and had not yet stopped, he could not blame overly bright sunbeams.

"A real duke," the groom breathed. "Fancy that."

"I am..." Callum paused, allowing himself to smile. His next words would change everything. "I am Callum Montgomery, Duke of Vernon."

Wonder was certainly supposed to be etched upon the woman's face now, but her countenance seemed curiously devoid of it. Her voice didn't wobble, and her gaze didn't flutter to her lap. In fact... She didn't seem to be the least bit intrigued.

Is it possible she hasn't heard of me?

Impressive headlines accompanied his depiction in broadsheets. "Wellington's Right Hand Man Halts Bonaparte," one had read, and then "...climbs the Matterhorn," and "...swims the channel." The latter two *might* be rumors, but Callum hadn't seen fit to correct them.

Naturally, some women were unacquainted with his many feats of brilliance. Those women, though, tended to be servants or other forms of workers who would not have the time to dedicate to perusing broadsheets. Some of them were of the older variety with failing eyes.

Old was not a word he would use to describe her.

Callum tried to remember the woman's name. She wasn't a servant, he could see that now. In fact, he was certain he'd seen her before.

Her name was something Butterworth. *Charlotte Butterworth.* She was a member of the *ton,* even if one of the most external rings.

He leaned back, proud of his memory. He contemplated sharing his knowledge with her, but since she would be well aware of her name, and since she already seemed disinclined to flattery, he doubted she would laud his memory, especially if he hinted her name was of such unimportance that recalling it demanded praise.

He'd never spoken to her, but he remembered the laughter that had accompanied the name. Apparently, the woman's father was a county vicar with no prospects of becoming even a deacon, but the woman's mother's blood was respectable, and she'd wrangled her daughters into the season, where they appeared mostly bewildered by their sumptuous surroundings and polished guests.

London was swarming with young women this time of year, even though the fabric of this woman's gown seemed suited for the garb of one of the more pious monk denominations, and her hair seemed curiously unbrushed. The hem of her dress didn't flare out in the modern way, and few ribbons adorned it.

Parliament was in session, and the season was in full force. The wives of the House of Lords hosted grand balls in their London townhouses, plotting to marry their children off to the wealthiest, most attractive people from the most distinguished families. In most cases, this meant their family members had mastered the art of plundering and fawning over the royal family centuries ago. In the autumn, these people would disappear to their vast manor homes and estates, reciting poetry in Grecian-style follies and playing the pianoforte, indulging in the luxuries secured by their husbands and fathers in the latest legislations.

Many women resembled her, though they were decidedly better dressed. This woman's blond locks and blue eyes were not precisely unappealing. Many women of the *ton* also had peaches-and-cream complexions and fair hair, signs perhaps of a Viking heritage, though none of them seemed prone to tearing out lungs from rib cages and draping them across their victims' shoulders in classic blood-eagle fashion. He eyed the woman's parasol, lest she take an old-fashioned attitude toward violence.

Callum rubbed his shoulder. He had never considered the advantages of parasols for serving as weapons, but from the manner she was pummeling him, it seemed obvious the British Army had neglected a weapon that would have ended the Napoleonic Wars earlier.

"You are going in the wrong direction," Miss Charlotte Butterworth said primly.

Callum would have disputed that fact. Wolfe was nowhere to be seen. It was clear he was very much going in the right direction.

Miss Butterworth pressed her lips together, and her skin seemed paler than before. "I need to return."

"To the Serpentine?" He scrunched his eyebrows together. Hyde Park was pleasant, but it was hardly the sort of place that demanded one visit at a certain time. The only requirement to see the Serpentine was to view it when it was light.

What exactly was Miss Butterworth intending to do? Have a secret rendezvous? He'd never imagined the vicar's daughter was so interesting.

"We have left Rotten Road. This lane leads north."

"You need to go somewhere."

"I thought I'd made that quite evident." She shoved a stray lock of hair behind her ear, and her slender fingers quivered.

He sighed. "I'll take you."

He turned the horses around and headed back.

"But isn't someone here who wants to hurt you?" she asked.

"I'll be brave." He grinned. He needn't tell her Wolfe was his best friend. It was the sort of statement that might make her question his urgent entrance into her conveyance. "What is your destination?"

"St. James Square."

He almost sputtered. Then it was a secret rendezvous. Most women of the *ton* lived in Mayfair, in grand townhouses, with their families. St. James Square was known for its multitude of bachelor apartments.

Callum steered the horses from the idyllic spot in which he'd found her toward the rather less idyllic location she wanted to go.

"You shouldn't be out by yourself," he said.

"I have Jerry."

"The groom? He looks scarcely thirteen. Hardly an effective guard."

"The circumstances were exceptional. Besides, no one was supposed to know."

"Your parents will miss you."

"It's early, and they have a tendency to enjoy the bed to the fullest."

"It's dangerous to travel on your own," he growled.

"I was in Hyde Park. Hardly Seven Dials."

"A woman like you isn't supposed to know what Seven Dials is."

She tossed her hair, and light blond tendrils fell from her bonnet. She shoved them back, tucking them under the coarse straw, and raised her chin. "I read."

"The broadsheets no doubt." The horses exited the park, and the cart jostled over cobblestones. Normally Callum might admire the buildings, so different from the Scottish Highlands, but he kept his gaze on her. "If I had any daughters, I wouldn't permit them to read any broadsheets."

"If you had any daughters my age, you would be a medical miracle," she retorted, and he fought the urge to smile. "Besides, what would you have them read now? And how would they know to avoid Seven Dials?"

He considered this, but before he could respond, she pointed.

"Stop there."

He urged the horses to the side of the pavement.

Obviously, the woman was seeing some man. In Callum's experience, a woman who desired a secret meeting desired a man, even if most women intent on meeting a man in private were prone to clothe themselves in more elegant attire. St. James Square was filled with men of venerable backgrounds and not venerable lifestyles; perfect for a woman driven by baser desires. He'd been the subject of many forbidden visits himself, and he grinned and directed his gaze at the building, wondering whether he knew the man to whom it belonged.

A plaque glimmered in the sunlight, and he read the name.

It was not what he'd expected.

Dr. William Hutton.

Callum stiffened.

In one respect, he was correct: she *was* seeing a man. The name Dr. William Hutton could hardly belong to a female, but it was the words underneath which caused Callum's stomach to tighten.

Heart physician.

This wasn't some illicit, sordid meeting. Perhaps the meeting was forbidden, but Callum had the impression the fact she was not accompanied by a family member or even a servant had less to do with protecting herself, than protecting them.

"What's this about?" Callum asked.

"Most likely nothing."

He doubted it was nothing.

In his experience, young ladies did not possess a habit of visiting heart physicians. If she was here, it was because she was concerned for her health.

And that is not good.

He scrutinized Miss Butterworth again, and she lowered her lashes. He straightened. He was being rude. He shouldn't scrutinize the shade of her pale skin or the slightness of her body. She didn't *seem* unwell.

But then hadn't his parents died suddenly after giving no indication of being vulnerable to illness?

That was different.

His stomach attempted to arrange itself into one of the more complex fisherman's knots, and he inhaled. He forced thoughts of his parents from his mind. Thoughts of his parents might lead to thoughts of his guardian on that dreadful afternoon, and he had no desire to linger on *that.*

Callum exited the cart. He turned to assist Miss Butterworth, but she was already striding briskly to the entrance.

"Pardon, Your Grace," the groom said. "I should take care of the horses."

"Er—naturally." Callum stepped away from the cart. The groom soon led the horses about the square, and Callum was alone.

He should leave. He should return to his townhouse on Grosvenor Square and resume some sleep before he made an appearance at Sir Seymour's ball this evening.

Except...

He didn't like the idea of Miss Butterworth making her way to her home herself, even if, despite the profusion of young men, it was unlikely danger would come to her at St. James's Square. The leafy squares and imposing residential homes were hardly cesspools of vice, and Miss Butterworth wouldn't be the first young lady of the *ton* to ride in these neighborhoods on her own. The less than one mile jaunt along the finest streets of the British Empire could hardly be termed terrifying.

A few of his friends streamed from their homes, decked in their top hats and canes, ready to amble to White's or other clubs in style. On any other day, he would have stopped to chat with them.

Today though he avoided their glances, consumed with the sense something of increased importance might be happening at the physician's.

Chapter Three

CHARLOTTE MARCHED TOWARD Dr. Hutton's office.

Perhaps if Charlotte had been another woman, her heart would have increased the frequency of its beats when the Duke of Vernon landed in her cart. His sudden arrival was the sort of thing less scientific minded women might have labeled fate. Perhaps then she would have imagined how her name would have looked beside his. Other girls were in the habit of doing this with men with whom they'd exchanged far fewer words.

Instead, the duke was only an annoyance; she was late. It had been difficult to secure an appointment, and more difficult to sneak from her home.

Charlotte inhaled. She couldn't have a problem.

It was ridiculous.

She had to be healthy. Had to be.

It wasn't unusual for people to see a physician, but usually the physician came to them. But it wouldn't do to worry Mama. She had enough things to worry about. Besides, this physician came highly recommended.

Charlotte opened the door and stepped inside. Marble tiles, arranged in geometric patterns of calcite and dolomite, covered the floor, like an easier-to-clean Persian carpet. Elaborate vases, a testament to the financial success of the physician's practice, crowned slender-legged sideboards. Landscape paintings in gilded frames lined the walls, though if they were placed to generate calm in the patients, they were ineffective for her. Charlotte's heart still swerved and swung inside her chest, as if at risk for toppling to the marble tile.

A young man sat at a desk. He hadn't been there when she last visited.

She inhaled and approached him, even though she despised meeting new people. "I'm here to see Dr. Hutton."

"Dr. Hutton has left."

"I-I had an appointment."

"Then you were late," the man said.

Lateness was an unusual pastime for her, and warmth descended up her cheeks, as if Satan himself were lighting them with embers from the underworld. "When will he be back?"

"One month," he said. "He's attending a very important conference in Scotland."

"Oh." Charlotte's shoulders sank, as if compelled by the same gravity that seemed inclined to tip over her heart. "Dr. Hutton's letter said I should come most urgently. Did he leave a message for me?"

"No."

Fiddle-faddle.

Charlotte had missed her important appointment. She didn't want to come back next month. It had been sufficiently horrible to visit Dr. Hutton's office this time.

She resisted the temptation to slink back through the door and squared her shoulders, even if the narrowness of their breadth was unlikely to be intimidating. The doctor's assistant must have information. A place like this would have documents in well-organized cabinets. "It's just, I had these chest pains..."

The man's eyes rounded, and a look of nervousness that seemed entirely novel came in. "Forgive me. You're Miss—er—Butter...?"

"Butterworth," she said.

A pained expression came over the man's face, and he raked his hand through his hair. "I'm Dr. Hutton's apprentice. I—er—didn't expect you to look so young. There was something he wanted to impart. Something—er—vital. Something not good."

"Not good?" Charlotte's voice wobbled.

"Indeed. Not good. Most—er—definitely not good." The man's gaze wandered about the hallway, as if searching for a fainting couch on which to place her. None existed of course, only the cold marble floor.

"I suppose I may as well tell you. No use you waiting. You'll want to leave soon." He emitted a laugh, but Charlotte had the impression he did not find what he was laughing at amusing, and the unpleasant feeling continued to gnaw on her heart.

Her heart always hurt when she worried, and sometimes, when everyone looked at her, she would gasp for breath. Georgiana and her parents said it was the way she was, but their hearts never hurt, and they never gasped for breath. Perhaps it was serious, just as she feared.

The apprentice inhaled, as if to calm himself, when she was certain the news would be unwelcome to *her*. "I am afraid you are going to die."

The man's voice, which had seemed unremarkable before, now seemed to possess the fortitude of thunder. *Die.* The word echoed in her mind.

She squeezed her eyes shut. He couldn't mean...*that.* "We will all die."

"But—er—your death will be soon. In a few months, in fact." He gave the same horrible, awkward laugh again. "You beat us."

"I-I don't understand." Something had seemed wrong, but the finality of the doctor's diagnosis shook her.

"Your heart pains are serious. Dr. Hutton said your death will be in a few months. At least you won't need to make Christmas presents."

I'm dying.

Her legs wobbled, and she clasped a nearby sideboard. The demi lune shape and Queen Anne legs scarcely seemed suitable for supporting its own weight, much less hers. The Oriental vase wobbled, a flurry of cranes and jagged mountains she would never see. She'd never even been on the ocean, and her heart tightened. The most independent thing she'd ever done was to venture here without her mother.

How will I tell her?

"Perhaps it's a mistake," Charlotte said. "It must be a mistake."

"I'm sorry," he said awkwardly. "But Dr. Hutton was quite clear."

Charlotte forced herself to nod. The physician was the best. Charlotte knew that. She'd researched him carefully beforehand.

"Can anything be done?" she asked finally, even though she knew the answer. If something could be done, he would have told her already.

The apprentice shook his head, but the action seemed as violent as if he'd jabbed a sword into her chest.

"Dr. Hutton recommended you get your affairs in order and to shield yourself from stress. Any excitement could be fatal." The apprentice had abandoned the papers on his desk and was scrutinizing her, as if calculating the likelihood she might steal the Oriental vase displayed on the sideboard or if she were simply susceptible to shattering it.

The air cooled, and if the apprentice spoke, she couldn't hear him. Life consisted only of the doctor's dreadful prognosis.

She wasn't supposed to die. Not yet. Not without decades and decades of glorious memories. Not without a husband, a child or two, and ideally grandchildren. That had been the plan.

But people died. People died every day. She simply hadn't believed she would belong to that category. Not yet.

Dr. Hutton's prognosis was unambiguous. She'd seen him for chest pains, and she'd been right to be concerned; her heart was malfunctioning.

She'd made an oversight in not considering she was approaching her death with a held in people whose total years numbered three digits.

Perhaps her life could be prolonged. Wouldn't an extra week, even an extra day be beneficial? Perhaps her parents might move to Bath. Wasn't that what other people might do in her situation? But the thought of spending all her time taking the cure, of being the youngest dying woman, of having strangers feel sorry for her—she despised that.

She couldn't stay here. She scrambled for the door and did her best not to stumble from the physician's office.

England had had terrible weather all year, but this morning rosy light splattered across the ivory facade of Dr. Hutton's building. Rosettes and cornices glowed under the uncharacteristic burst of sun rays. Birds darted on their wings against the clear blue sky and chirped to one another in cheerful tones, as if to remind her life was good, and she wouldn't experience it for much longer.

I don't want to die.

She quickened her pace and attempted to keep her face calm, before the finely-attired men and women of the *ton* who paraded the square. She managed to keep her chin parallel with the ground, but she found herself blinking, and her eyes burned.

"Miss Butterworth?" The duke's voice interrupted her musings, and she widened her eyes. The duke was leaning nonchalantly against the cart.

"You're still here," she said.

"Yes."

"You didn't have to remain."

In fact—she'd rather he *hadn't*. She was in no mood to make small talk with him.

THE WOMAN SEEMED RATHER less confident than she'd been when she'd entered the physician's office. Though Callum would have liked to have credited her pale face and quivering gait to a belated recognition of the handsomeness of his features and significance of his title, Callum feared that was not the case.

Her gait lacked its earlier confidence. Her movements were languid, and her face inscrutable.

"Is everything fine?" he asked.

She gave a quick smile, no doubt intended to dismiss him, for her eyes did not sparkle, and Callum noted she had not answered his question.

"You needn't have waited for me," she said finally.

"I know."

"Or did you desire to be driven somewhere else? Hacks function quite well and come with much less scandal."

"I'm aware of the wonders of hacks," he said, refraining from admitting his experience with them was minimal.

Dukes had a variety of carriages from which to choose, but the list did not generally include vehicles for hire.

"You should go," she said.

Callum considered her words. He had no desire for scandal. If he had any sense, he would have scampered off long ago. At this rate, one of her parents might shout "compromised," and he would find himself engaged to her within the week. The engagement with Lady Isla sufficed in intolerability.

The last thing he desired was to have her father come after him. Vicars had a well-developed sense of right and wrong, and he was certain her father would consider spending time with his unmarried daughter was decidedly in the wrong category.

Still, he lingered.

Something about her demeanor seemed to have shifted, as if she were on the verge of collapsing. Her face was damned pale.

"Did you have bad news?"

"It's of no concern to you." Miss Butterworth's expression remained calm and controlled, but her eyes didn't meet his, and he was certain she was swaying.

Damnation.

The news seemed very much to concern her.

He wasn't going to allow her to faint on the pavement. What on earth had the doctor told her?

"Let me talk with the doctor," he said.

Her eyes widened, and perhaps she would have protested, but he brushed past her. He strode toward the building. The ivory exterior seemed innocuous, and he glared at the Grecian goddesses perched on the facade, smug in their immortality.

"Your Grace! You mustn't!" Miss Butterworth called, and he assumed the footsteps scampering behind him were hers.

He quickened his pace, pushed open the door and stepped into a hallway.

"Sir?" A young man, most likely an apprentice, eyed him suspiciously. Most likely the man had a sufficient familiarity with his schedule to know Callum was not expected.

"It's, Your Grace," Callum said shortly. "I am the Duke of Vernon."

"Your Grace?" The apprentice sputtered, and his cheeks pinkened in a manner that emphasized his youth. "Truly?"

"Truly," Miss Charlotte Butterworth said miserably, entering the building.

Callum was not prone to announcing his title and prestige to workers, but this was the sort of occasion that demanded it.

"Forgive me, Your Grace," the apprentice said.

Callum had no interest in seeing how much the apprentice's once rigid posture might collapse. The man's grovel was unnecessary, and he firmed his expression. "I demand you tell me what you said to that young lady."

"You mustn't do that," Miss Butterworth exclaimed.

"Tell me," Callum said sternly.

"Are you a relative?" the apprentice asked.

"He most certainly is not," Miss Butterworth said.

"She's my betrothed," Callum lied, and Miss Butterworth's eyebrows jolted up. She seemed momentarily too stunned to say anything. *Good.*

"I am afraid..." The apprentice's voice croaked. "She's going to...die."

"Die?"

The man nodded vigorously, as if pleased to have gotten the word out. "Quite soon. A few months."

Callum's stomach again attempted an elaborate knot, and he turned to Miss Butterworth's pale, brave face. "But you're young. This must be a mistake."

"I did expect more years." Miss Butterworth rested a quivering hand on her chest. "Yet statistically it is not impossible I should be one of those people to die early."

"But your health—"

"—Worried me sufficiently that I came here."

He was silent. He didn't know her. He shouldn't be arguing over this.

"I should never have shared this with you," she said.

She was correct.

People died all the time. 0

How long had his parents lived? How old had Aunt Edwina been when she'd passed?

That was different.

He turned to the apprentice. "Perhaps the doctor made a mistake."

"The physician does not make mistakes." The man had the unctuousness and slavish attention found in men of lesser position. "Dr. Hutton attended *Paris University*."

Callum hoped he'd done so before the war. It did not speak to the man's judgement to study in the country of Britain's main enemy.

"If he says it's correct—"

"—Then it must be correct," Callum grumbled.

"Quite," the apprentice said.

"And where exactly is the physician?" Callum asked.

"On his way to Edinburgh." The apprentice's eyes glimmered. "The physician is attending a most important conference."

Callum had previously expressed pride at Edinburgh's reputation as a center for medicine. He rather wished now that London had exerted itself more. He was hardly going to go to Edinburgh to question the validity of a doctor's diagnosis.

Not that it would have been any use. The physician would hardly have told Miss Charlotte Butterworth her life would be sharply curtailed unless he was certain. Even a man educated in Paris could find no amusement in that.

My parents died.

The room's temperature soared, as if placed in the Sahara, and sweat prickled the back of his neck. Callum yanked his cravat, and the apprentice widened his eyes. Most likely the venerable Dr. Hutton never yanked his cravat. Callum's legs wobbled, as if he were not only in the Sahara, but experiencing a sandstorm.

Miss Charlotte Butterworth's blue eyes rounded. "Are you well, Your Grace?"

"Er—naturally." Callum wasn't dying after all. He forced himself to straighten and maintain some semblance of dignity. "I'll see you to the carriage, Miss Butterworth."

"That is unnecessary," she said primly and hurried from the building.

Chapter Four

CHARLOTTE SCURRIED into her family's small, dimly lit townhouse. Though she had perfected the art of walking as a small child and practiced it regularly with brisk afternoon strolls, her legs quivered. Her stomach toppled about, as if she were on a sinking ship.

I should tell them.

Charlotte had read penny novels. She knew how death worked. Usually the most angelic person in the family died. Though Charlotte would hardly term herself angelic, her family members did so with incorrigible frequency, imbuing her with lofty qualities, merely because she possessed an interest in books. If they knew she were ill, her family might bustle her off to Bath or Harrogate, abandoning Georgiana's last season and any hope for securing their finances. When they weren't thrusting her into water with other sick people, they might be huddling about her bed in a maudlin manner.

No.

Charlotte had no urge to tell them.

"Oh, Charlotte! Charlotte, dear!" Mama's voice soared through the townhouse. Its unfashionable age might have come with thick walls, but no amount of stone could obstruct her mother's natural *fortissimo.*

"Yes?" Charlotte squeaked. Had her mother noticed her absence? Been pacing the house? Sent a search party for her?

"Did I show you the new ribbons I selected from the haberdasher?"

Relief cascaded through Charlotte, and she entered the drawing room. Books bulged from bookcases. The townhouse was small, and Papa did not have a separate library. He sat in one corner, contentedly perusing his philosophy. Mama and Georgiana sat on the sofa.

Mama waved green ribbons in each hand. "I want to use one of the ribbons for my dress tonight, but I'm not sure which one."

Charlotte had seen the ribbons before. Her mother had shown them to her. Both pomona and pistache were unlikely combinations with her mother's capucine ball gown. Green and orange was a combination best appreciated in carrots.

"You don't need any ribbons on your dress, my dear. You always look lovely." Charlotte's father kissed Mama on her cheek.

Mama giggled. "You silly man. Isn't he silly, Charlotte?"

Charlotte nodded and forced herself to smile. Her face felt stiff, numb from the visit to the doctor.

I'm dying.

She'd repeated the sentence in her mind, as if it were some chant. But unlike a call to some religion, asking for better crops, there was no hope for salvation. There would never be. Her heart was failing, and by the end of the year, she would be gone.

It was enough to make her want to sprint toward her mother, despite the furniture, despite the fact that her stiff stays rendered sudden movements uncomfortable, and despite the fact that she hadn't run to her mother's arms in over a decade.

She resisted the temptation. How could she burden her parents with that dreadful prognosis? She hardly comprehended it herself.

"Your dear mother has received an invitation to go to a ball," Papa said.

Oh.

"We've *all* received the invitation," Mama corrected. "Imagine? Me going on my own? How scandalous."

"You'll always be my scandal." Papa kissed Mama's hand, and their eyes glimmered at each other.

Normally Charlotte might roll her eyes, but now her heart ached. No one would ever look at her with such love.

Love, like visiting the ocean, would be another thing she would never experience.

"You're making Charlotte look ill," Georgiana exclaimed, and her parents halted their expressions of affection.

"I'm quite fine," Charlotte protested.

At least, it wasn't her *parents* who caused her distress.

"Of course she is," Mama said. "She's going to a ball."

Mama's lips were fixed into a wide smile others might reserve for visiting a beloved, seldom-seen relative. Though they'd been in London for the entirety of the season, balls remained a special occasion. Despite Mama's birth and the lofty positions of her relatives, much of the *ton* seemed suspicious of Charlotte and Georgiana.

Mama seemed so happy.

How could Charlotte confide in her?

I won't.

Not now. Not when Mama seemed to think there was a possibility Georgiana or Charlotte would marry well.

I'll have my normal day.

"Whose ball are we going to?" Charlotte asked.

"Lady Amberly!" Mama clapped her hands, and the ribbons on her lace cap swung, as if held by some exuberant Maypole dancer.

Georgiana blinked. "The Duchess of Alfriston?"

Mama shook her hand. "No, no. That would be quite impossible. The Duchess of Alfriston is no longer an Amberly. She is a Carmichael now. But Lady Amberly is her aunt, and her husband is a baronet," Mama said.

"So not *so* impressive."

"She has an unmarried son of eligible age," Mama said.

"I rather expect there will be more than one unmarried man of eligible age in attendance," Papa said dryly.

Mama clapped her hands again. "Oh, indeed! But think, one of our daughters could become the wife of a baronet, could become the mother of a baronet."

"The grandmother of a baronet?" Papa suggested, and Mama's eyelashes fluttered.

Papa set down his Hegel. "Your mother went to school with Lady Amberly."

"Truly?" Georgiana asked.

"Indeed," Mama said. "So you'll be sure to get an introduction. I believe a duke will be there as well, but I didn't go to school with him."

"That would have been quite scandalous," Papa said. "Imagine her wearing one of those top hats and sneaking into Eton?"

Charlotte crossed her legs. She'd once dreamed of doing just such a thing, and her skin warmed at the memory of the girlish daydream.

"Charlotte, you must wear pink," Mama said. "Pink is the very best color for you."

"I'll resemble a giant flower," Charlotte said.

Mama scrutinized her, and the ribbons on her cap halted their ceaseless movement. "That is exactly the point, my dear."

"Men are not known for delighting in flowers," Charlotte said.

Her sister Georgiana adored flowers and gardens, but conversations on the merits of wisteria and willow trees seemed unlikely to draw most men from their discussions on army maneuvers. Men weren't known to go about plucking wildflowers, and they didn't spend all afternoon creating their likenesses in needlepoint.

"Such naivety, my dear," Mama said. "Everyone adores flowers, even though not all of them might admit it. Besides, your skin is so fair, but when you wear pink, your cheeks and lips manage to look becoming. For a woman who is as intelligent as you are, you do not know very much."

Charlotte frowned. That explanation sounded almost logical.

"It doesn't matter what I wear," Charlotte said finally. "It's my first season."

"And Georgiana's third," Mama said quietly.

Charlotte turned her head toward her mother.

Mama wasn't in the habit of expressing anything but the most jubilant enthusiasm about the virtues of her children, but she must be cognizant of the gossips. Charlotte had not paid much attention to their chit-chat. She was the second daughter of a vicar. Her mother had married inappropriately, and her relatives on her mother's side were determined Charlotte not make a similar mistake.

"Still." Mama beamed. "Perhaps you will meet a duke."

Charlotte stiffened, remembering the duke she'd met that morning.

"That would be unlikely," Charlotte said. "Statistically improbable."

"I imagine you're correct, dear," Mama said.

"He's tall, blond and handsome." Mama's eyes gleamed. "And his accent has a Scottish burr."

Is it...him?

She frowned. She'd never expected to see the duke again. The man knew far too much about her. If only he hadn't wrangled that information from Dr. Hutton's apprentice.

Not that it would matter if they attended the same ball. He was certain to be beset by matchmaking mamas and desperate debutantes. Even Mama would admit dukes were rather too grand for someone like Georgiana or her to consider, especially ones in possession of all their teeth.

Charlotte rose. "I'll work on Papa's books."

"Numbers aren't feminine, my dear," Mama said.

"I wasn't aware soldiers carried abacuses to war," Georgiana said.

Mama adjusted her hair in the mirror. "You haven't been to war, darling."

Charlotte turned away. She couldn't compete with her mother and sister. They sparred all day. Their dialogue was quick and witty. Even though her sister would make exasperated noises around her mother, their similarities were evident.

"Ah, let her do them," Papa said, smoothing the cream colored pages of his tome. "Saves me the trouble."

"Thank you, Papa," Charlotte said.

She needed something with which to distract her mind. Charlotte was good at numbers. Numbers made sense. One could add and subtract them. Multiply and divide them. And they always acted predictably.

People were much less predictable. Mother frequently wailed about something, and though Father tended more toward quiet, with the exception of those days in which he was preaching at his pulpit, she was not truly similar to him. Philosophy books held no interest to her—not like numbers.

People seemed to expect her to say the right words to them. They would ask questions and then not like her answers. People were confusing.

Charlotte had learned early on that *not* saying what was on her mind was almost certainly the appropriate thing to do. She was reserved.

Numbers, with their propensity for behaving in an orderly fashion, while often arranging themselves into new combinations, were beautiful.

Chapter Five

CALLUM MONTGOMERY PACED Sir Seymour's ballroom. The ball succeeded in encapsulating everything he most abhorred about London and the *ton.* At least he was not at Almack's and forced into a ridiculous outfit, mandated by the patronesses' allegiance to anything out-of-date, as if their guests had joined a large monkey zoo.

"Ah, Your Grace!" Sir Seymour dashed toward him, elbowing his way through the throng of guests. His high heels clattered against the polished floor. The shoes were less likely an adherence to outdated fashion than a desire to make himself taller. The baronet stopped before Callum and gave a deep bow. "I am most honored you would join us."

"It is my pleasure," Callum said.

In truth, he hadn't wanted another night at the club. His concerns with Wolfe seemed trifling after meeting Miss Charlotte Butterworth. At least he hadn't been told he suffered a fatal illness.

"My wife will be most delighted," Sir Seymour said. "We have invited a special guest for you."

"Bagpipe entertainment?" Callum jested, uncertain what precisely the baronet would consider a special guest for him.

Sir Seymour flushed. "Not bagpipe entertainment. I-I hadn't realized your great interest. But you're Scottish, so of course I see I should—"

Callum took pity on the man's stammering. "Please do not worry." He leaned closer to the baronet. "I haven't visited Scotland in years."

Sir Seymour beamed and he straightened. "And the noise bagpipes produce is horrendous."

"That is not true," Callum said tersely.

Even though Callum hadn't returned to Scotland since the war and was considered English by many, he despised listening to the English mock his homeland. His wariness of Scotland derived from his childhood memories of his guardian, not any lack of affection for the place itself, no matter what others assumed.

Callum exhaled and reminded himself that the baronet was attempting to be pleasant, even if Sir Seymour's effort resulted in rudeness.

Memories of Miss Butterworth drifted through Callum's mind. She'd been so much herself, unbeholden to anyone and without any vanity. She'd been...refreshing.

Her family must be devastated. Most likely she was tucked away in her bed.

He forced himself to listen to Sir Seymour. Death happened. He'd learned that early.

"I'll give you a tour of the townhouse," Sir Seymour said. "I have many guests, but you, Your Grace, exceed them in importance."

"I'm certain all of them are important."

"Nonsense. You're the only duke." Sir Seymour grinned and waved to a footman, who swiftly approached. "Give His Grace a drink."

The footman lowered his silver platter of coquelicot colored drinks, and Callum took one.

"Now be off, young man," Sir Seymour said to the footman. "No dallying here."

The footman's complexion took on a ruddy tint, and he strode backward, as if he'd mistaken Sir Seymour for the mad king.

"Please, Your Grace, allow me to show you some paintings I snapped up for a steal," Sir Seymour said, once again jovial. "My neighbor, the esteemed late Lord Mulbourne, was a great art collector. After his death, his heir sold me some of his art for a very good price."

"I gather you do not appreciate the finery of paintings," Callum said.

"I do not," Sir Seymour said. "How a man could spend time creating something that does not exist is beyond me. Utter waste of time."

"Perhaps landscapes appeal to you more."

"Landscapes are the creation of people who do not have the sense to look out the window," Sir Seymour huffed. "Complete frivolity."

"Not everyone is as fortunate as you are to have a home in the countryside."

"But do those people matter? They don't even belong to the House of Lords." Sir Seymour shook his head. "But my dear son Cecil assures me art can be most valuable. I am fond of good investments. Nothing brings pleasure like money."

Callum resisted the urge to ask why Sir Seymour spent so much time gambling in Hades' Lair.

Sir Seymour's musicians played country dances, though the dancers moved stiffly. The punch had a decidedly nonalcoholic taste and was hardly conducive to festivity.

"I should mingle with other people," Callum suggested. "I would not like to occupy all of your time. You are the host and you have a great many guests."

"I have, haven't I?" Sir Seymour grinned and leaned closer to Callum. "I didn't serve real alcohol. All about economizing, that's what I say. If it's good enough for Almack's, it's good enough for me."

Callum almost smiled.

In fact, he was certain he might have, but the scent of a certain perfume wafted near him, and he stiffened. "Lord Seymour? Who exactly is the surprise guest?"

"Ah," Sir Seymour beamed. "She is standing behind you." The baronet leaned closer. "I am quite romantic. When I learned she was in town, I said to myself, 'Seymour, you have got to invite her to your ball.'"

Callum turned his head and Lady Isla stood before him.

"Is any woman more beautiful than your betrothed?" Sir Seymour said appreciatively. "Not my wife, that's for certain. You're a lucky man, Your Grace."

Lady Isla gave a slow smile,

She was beautiful; anyone could see that, and people remarked on the fact frequently. Her dark hair was shaped into an immaculate chignon, and every lock was coiled. Her green eyes gleamed, accentuating the emeralds that adorned her throat. Her gown must be Parisian, and the navy color emanated sophistication.

"Lady Isla." He bowed deeply. Callum supposed he was lucky, but perhaps because he'd been practically raised in her nursery, he felt no passion toward her.

"My dear Duke." Amusement tinged her alto voice, and he wondered if his discomfort was evident. "I'd expected to meet you earlier."

"A ballroom is more appropriate than a gaming hell," he said.

"And it's my ballroom," Sir Seymour said, interrupting the conversation with a gleeful clap of his hands. "I hope this earns me a wedding invitation."

"I'm certain that could be arranged," Lady Isla said smoothly.

Blast.

Lady Isla shouldn't be giving out invitations to their wedding. There had to be some confirmation process. Her father couldn't simply declare them engaged when they were seven.

"You should have a large wedding," Sir Seymour said. "St. George's Chapel is most convenient. I always tell my boy Cecil he should marry there when he finally becomes betrothed."

"Large weddings are typically the habit of royalty."

"And you, Vernon, are a duke."

"I quite agree," Lady Isla said. "Large festivities are so much more momentous."

Callum gave a tight smile.

The strains of a waltz played, and Lady Isla looked at him expectedly. "I do enjoy dancing."

"Then you must ask the lady to dance," Sir Seymour exclaimed. "A man with such a beautiful woman should be twirling her about. I assure you, your attire will look very becoming against these marble floors."

Callum descended quickly into a bow. Perhaps that way Lady Isla would not see the manner in which his face was tightening. Lord McIntyre *had* assisted his family, and he should not be so open in his reservations against marrying Lady Isla. There could be far worse wives than her. Everyone said so.

"May I have this dance?" he murmured.

Murmurings sounded, and every gaze seemed directed at them.

Lady Isla smirked and stretched out her hand to him. "We're a magnificent couple."

Callum nodded. People had been marveling at the appropriateness of their match since they were children. Lady Isla had exuded perfection then, mastering each melody on the pianoforte with Edwina.

He led her effortlessly about the ballroom, and they glided together. She'd been his first ballroom partner, though their dance tutor no longer shouted advice from the corner of Lord McIntyre's great hall.

"You left abruptly this morning," Isla said.

"I had an appointment," he lied.

"Where did you go?"

"The doctor's."

She blinked. Evidently, she hadn't expected that answer. "You're unwell?"

"Me?" He squeaked. "No, no. I'm healthy. Fit as a fiddle."

Her perfect eyes narrowed, and he busied himself with covering more space on the ballroom floor.

"I'd rather you hadn't invited him to the wedding," Callum said.

"You desire more privacy?"

Callum hesitated.

For a moment, he considered telling her he didn't want to marry her, and that he had no desire to honor the old earl's wishes.

Would she understand? Or would she simply defend her father and tell him Callum had indeed killed his parents by giving them the pox? Would she laugh and call him childish for still being upset? Would she even repeat her father's claim that Callum had dreamed his aunt's presence?

Perhaps no one would believe him and she would tell all the world he was displaying lunatic tendencies.

He darted his gaze about the ballroom, sweat prickling his brow, but the waltz did not make it convenient for him to wipe it away.

A flash of blond hair caught his eyes.

Miss Charlotte Butterworth.

The chit was bravely sipping Sir Seymour's punch, even though she should be in bed. Instead, she was attired in a pink gown in which her slender figure seemed lost.

"You missed a step," Isla interrupted his musings.

"I'm—er—sorry," he said.

"You never miss a step." Isla arched her exquisitely plucked eyebrows, and her emerald eyes rounded. "What has happened to you?"

He squared his shoulders and forced himself to concentrate on the dance. Their bodies soon swayed in rhythm. No woman was more confident on the ballroom floor, and some of the other dancers had paused their waltzes to gaze at them.

"They're looking at us," Isla murmured.

The ballroom thinned, and Callum's view of Miss Charlotte Butterworth improved. She was all by herself. What would compel her, in her state, to go to a ball and stand in a corner? The inner workings of the woman flummoxed him.

"Callum," Isla whispered. "You're not focused."

"I—er..." Callum always danced well. That was one of his good qualities. Everyone remarked on it. Men couldn't hide imperfect steps behind long gowns. Their legs were always on display.

Isla narrowed her eyes and craned her head behind her. "But that's only a room corner with a single wallflower in it." She returned her gaze to him. "I thought the regent must have wandered in."

"I believe he's in Brighton. Maybe you could see him there."

"At least he tells interesting stories," Isla said.

"Which he makes up," Callum said.

"Hmph." Isla might have said more, but the dance ended. She gave him an elegant curtsy, and he remembered to bow.

"Excuse me," he told Isla, vaguely conscious of her eyebrows rising in surprise, before he wove through the room.

He brushed past middle-aged women sporting turbans and their daughters. On another occasion, Callum might have asked them to dance. This time he moved swiftly past them.

Finally, he found Miss Charlotte Butterworth. She'd managed to drink half her punch, a progress which could only have been unpleasant.

"What on earth are you doing here?" he demanded.

"Your Grace?"

"You should be in bed," he continued. "Where are your parents? I should speak with them. Your heart—"

"My heart is none of your concern," she said quickly. "I beg you to lower your voice."

The chit should be grateful he'd expressed concern, but instead her eyes were flashing with something resembling anger.

Callum sighed. "Are you feeling well?"

"I'm fine."

He scrutinized her. She didn't look fine. Her face was pale, and sweat shone on her brow.

"You should be in bed," he said.

"N-nonsense."

"Why not?"

"I'm quite capable of walking."

"I should speak with your parents," he grumbled.

She pale blue eyes widened.

"They're not taking care of you properly. Do they even know about your condition?"

She averted her eyes, and anger burst through him.

"Damnation."

"People are looking at us," she said.

"Let's dance then."

She blinked.

"You're at a ball. You mustn't look so surprised. It is rather what one does here."

"It's never been what *I* do there," she said softly.

He assessed her. "You're a wallflower."

She nodded.

"You know that doesn't mean you should be actually trying to blend in with the wall?"

A mauve color flooded her cheeks. "Naturally I'm aware that's only an expression..."

"Come, let's dance," he said gently. Dancing was something he knew how to do. Conversation was not required when dancing.

"I'm not very good," Charlotte said.

He gave her a reassuring smile. "I'm sure you're plenty good. You just have to follow the music."

"That's what everyone says," Charlotte said, and her voice seemed almost mournful.

"You look very pretty."

The words failed to dismiss the growing look of horror on her face.

"You're supposed to say 'thank you.' And perhaps even 'yes.'" Callum gave her his arm and led her onto the dance floor.

Chapter Six

THE DUKE GAZED AT HER in a strange manner, and she shivered. Men like him weren't supposed to gaze at women like her. Men like him were with the very finest women, who'd gone to the most immaculate finishing schools and who never appeared like they were drowning in their attire. Such women wore immaculate gowns with lace made by multiple workers over months that were embroidered with jewels mined from minerals in faraway caves and with vibrant colors taken from similarly precious dye, exported from faraway countries.

No.

Men like the Duke of Vernon were not supposed to pay any attention to women like Charlotte.

The countryside might be known for rosy-cheeked milkmaids, but Charlotte was too thin and pale to resemble them. Other women fretted over the unbecomingness of empire waist gowns, and the propensity of the high waist line to give the impression of impending motherhood. Charlotte never had those fears, though she'd been too short to conjure visions of Grecian regality that the designers intended.

Charlotte might have technically attended balls, but no matter her mother's ability to procure invitations, and no matter her mother's lineage, the fact remained Charlotte was not only the daughter, but also the second daughter, of a vicar.

It was the sort of occupation one might not truly be able to criticize, not like that of a fisherman or some other laborer, but she was certain it was an occupation they could hardly respect. After all, they were independently wealthy.

Finally the duke swept into a deep bow. "May I have this dance?"

She stared at him, unaccustomed to this new formality.

He leaned closer to her. "This is a ball, Miss Butterworth. The prospect of dancing can't be entirely baffling."

"B-but you're a duke," she stammered.

His lips twitched. "You seemed to give the indication earlier you found that less than impressive."

He led her to the row of finely attired people waiting to begin the dance, and she took his arm again, conscious of the startled expression on people's faces as they saw them together.

"I'm a terrible dancer," she warned.

His lips twitched again. "I rather much doubt it."

"You are a man of entirely too much optimism."

"Is that a quality I should be worried about?"

She assessed him. "I think it's a quality you should pride yourself in."

The duke blinked, obviously surprised, and she averted her gaze.

The dance needed to begin.

At any moment, she was going to transform into a perfectly simpering woman, whose every word to him was a compliment, and he'd think her despondent once he shifted his attention elsewhere.

MISS BUTTERWORTH WAS a terrible dancer.

The thin material of Callum's dance slippers was not an effective barricade against the frequency of her habit to step upon his toes.

"I told you I was dreadful," Miss Butterworth said.

"So you did," he said, doing his best to maintain a placid expression as his large toe throbbed with pain.

"I'm not in the habit of lying," she declared.

"Most admirable of you."

The music was particularly jaunty, but Miss Butterworth's lips were pursed in obvious concentration. Every now and then her lips would move, like some medieval witch about to utter a spell.

"Are you counting?" he asked.

"Doesn't everyone count when dancing?"

"I suppose at one time..."

"You must speak quickly," she said. "In fourteen seconds we are to be divided."

"I suppose you don't love dancing."

"I rather implied that," she said, and they separated.

No one stepped on Callum's foot when he joined a new pattern of dancers, but he was relieved when he rejoined her. "I thought you were being modest," he said, when they rejoined one another.

She shrugged. "Then you were mistaken. It's happened before with you. I imagine it is one of your characteristics."

"Being mistaken?"

She nodded seriously. "Logic is a subject with which some people struggle."

"But do not worry, there are subjects with which I struggle." She stepped on his toe again.

"I believe you."

Her face was grave and serious. She hadn't once mentioned ribbons or hinted at her strong capabilities for manor house management.

She'd been acting bravely, sipping atrocious punch, and lingering far too near the wall. The fact intrigued him. Bravery was something which he'd associated with troops in battle, but most of the women of his acquaintance were squeamish over something as trivial as a stray spider that ventured inside the house.

He wished the musicians had not just played a waltz. He wouldn't have been entirely disinclined to twirl about with her, and he was sad when the dance ended.

"How honorable of you to dance with our most incorrigible wallflowers," a man's voice said.

Sir Seymour.

Callum tried to temper the wave of irritation that rushed through his body.

"Your slippers must be in a sorry state," Sir Seymour continued, and Miss Butterworth's face pinkened. "His Grace is most kind, do you not feel? Especially when his own betrothed is at this ball?"

A pained expression appeared on her face.

Blast.

The point of asking Miss Butterworth to dance had *not* been to embarrass her.

"My slippers are fine," Callum said tightly.

"Ah," Sir Seymour said. "I imagine they are, given their ducal quality. You must share the name of your cobbler. Your taste is magnificent." He gave a quick glance at Miss Butterworth, and Callum doubted the baronet thought Miss Butterworth's taste magnificent. "But you are perhaps too noble, Your Grace. Perhaps it is a Scottish inclination. Your people never did manage to win the wars."

Callum stiffened. "War is not the only thing worth winning."

"Ah, but does one desire to live in an occupied country?" Sir Seymour mused. "All those times France tried to attack *us,* they never managed to, did they?"

"With the exception of the Normans conquering England in 1066," Miss Butterworth said tersely, and Callum gave a short laugh.

"It has been a pleasure dancing with you, Miss Butterworth." Callum swept into a deep bow, noting that Sir Seymour's face took on a purple shade.

Perhaps Callum's bow had been lower than absolutely necessary, but he had enjoyed their dance.

Miss Butterworth gave a not-particularly-elegant curtsy, but Callum expected Sir Seymour's glower might be unnerving. Callum had the advantage of being the object to Sir Seymour's awkward attempts at adulation.

Even though his valet might complain when he saw Callum's slippers, Callum felt almost a sense of regret when Miss Butterworth left.

Chapter Seven

THE DANCE HAD BEEN glorious, and now it was over. The evening was not supposed to be spent swirling in the arms of a duke. It was a strange variation from joining the other wallflowers, where the most exciting part of the evening was nibbling on the stale cake the patronesses offered and discussing fish with Miss Louisa Carmichael.

Charlotte departed from the duke. No need for him to continue to make conversation with her. The man was engaged, and his fiancée was present, somewhere, at this ball. The duke wasn't the first man who felt compelled to dance with some wallflowers. When he wasn't hopping into carriages which didn't belong to him, the man could behave quite nobly.

She spotted her mother's feathered turban in the throng of people and headed toward her. Perhaps Mama could distract her. Even though she despised dancing, memories of the man's hand on her waist and of his masculine scent still rushed through her mind.

"Did you see the duke dancing with that vicar's daughter?" a female voice behind her asked.

Tension sprang through Charlotte's body, as if attempting to transform her to stone, and the act of walking became difficult. She didn't recognize the sound of the voice. Whoever was speaking about her was no friend.

"Is that who she was?" asked a new, equally unpleasant voice with a slight Scottish burr. "I wonder she was allowed into this ballroom.

"This is hardly Almack's," the first woman said. "The baronet is happy to fill the ballroom with any guests. We are speaking about someone from *Yorkshire*."

"Evidently, even that county is vastly superior to wherever that girl was from. She was so dreadful at dancing."

The two women laughed, seemingly pleased in their open contempt.

Charlotte wrapped her arms against her chest. Her gloves scratched her, and her shift seemed too tight.

She glanced toward her mother's feathered turban. She had no desire to make conversation now. Where was Georgiana? Not that she could confide in her. Her sister had the habit of acting without thinking, and Charlotte wouldn't be surprised if Georgiana marched up to those despicable women and admonished them, turning the whole event into something even more unpleasant.

A slight flutter of wind brushed against her as she passed velvet drapes. *I can go outside.* It might be cold, but it would be private.

And privacy was exactly what she required.

Charlotte slipped behind the velvet curtain. The brocade pattern scratched against her face. Its elegance did not extend to its texture.

The space behind the curtain was dark, and she felt frigid glass beneath her gloves. She fumbled for a door knob, but there was no handle. Just a partway opened window, and one with no view.

Heat prickled her cheeks, even though no one was around to witness her. Had people seen her duck behind the curtain? They would think her ludicrous.

They already do.

She should leave now, but her chest tightened. At any moment, her breaths might come overly rapidly, and she would utterly humiliate herself. She shut her eyes. *I cannot remain here.*

"There you are, Vernon," one of the unpleasant women said. Her alto voice sounded impossibly loud. She must be standing on the other side of the curtain.

Charlotte shrank back. Any urge to step from the curtain vanished. She couldn't provide more gossip fodder. Her poor dancing and unfashionable attire had already sufficed in making this woman think herself superior.

"Lady Isla." A tenor voice with a slight Scottish accent sounded.

Charlotte didn't have to peer around the curtain to know whom the voice belonged to; it was the duke's.

"You disappeared. Is that how you treat your betrothed?"

The duke was engaged to this woman? Who criticized Charlotte within hearing difference? Who laughed about her with a friend? Who evidently belonged to the very highest strata of the *ton?*

Charlotte stiffened.

She felt ridiculous for pondering the symmetry of his facial features and the broadness of his chest. She felt ridiculous for contemplating the manner the golden candlelight hit his strands, making it gleam, and she certainly felt ridiculous for spending any amount of time with him. He was the cream of the peerage and she was...not.

"You do know you could have danced with me," Lady Isla said.

"A second dance in a row?" the duke asked. "I would not want to be scandalous."

"Nonsense. Our betrothal is no secret," Lady Isla said. "Not even the most etiquette conscious person would object to a second dance."

The duke was silent.

"You scampered toward that vicar's daughter with such speed. Anyone would think you'd decided to take up exercising in our dear host's ballroom." Lady Isla laughed, and the sound was melodic, even though nothing else about her seemed pleasant. "And after all, she is so *plain.*"

This was a private conversation.

This was not meant for her to hear.

Charlotte's stomach twisted, and she stepped closer to the window. The condensation prickled her sleeves. No doubt her puffed sleeves were turning a different color.

Fiddle-faddle.

She stepped away, and hoped no one noticed the curtain moving.

"Perhaps slenderness is fashionable," Lady Isla continued, "but she is *skinny*, and that height—it's not the least impressive. She scarcely fit into her gown."

"I don't take my lessons on beauty from what some magazine happens to say is fashionable, especially when the magazine has a definite interest in changing frequently."

"Hmph. Let's discuss our wedding instead of the tiresome women at second-rate balls," Lady Isla said. "We could have an August wedding."

"Is that your wish?" Callum's voice was collected, but even through the curtains, Charlotte could hear his voice wobble. The man seemed to radiate tension and unease.

Charlotte drew back. Her heart sped, sending blood through her body frantically, as if it thought itself some mill near a waterfall.

This was an imperfect hiding spot. The proper thing of course would be to saunter past Lady Isla and the duke. But sauntering past them might lead to questions as to why she'd been there in the first place, and that was something she had no desire to do.

"Yoo-who! Charlotte dear!" Her mother's voice sailed through the air, undeterred by Sir Seymour's curtains.

Charlotte stiffened and resisted the urge to inhale a deep breath, even as her heartbeat quickened, and even as thoughts of the general frailness of her heart assaulted her.

She would not permit herself to be discovered behind the curtain. Not when the duke and the impossibly beautiful, impossibly elegant Lady Isla were on the other side. She had no desire to see Lady Isla's eyebrow arch with amusement at her presence again, and she didn't want to ponder the duke's possible reaction to evidence of her eavesdropping.

"Charlotte, dear! I have someone for you to meet!" her mother's voice exclaimed.

Footsteps sounded, and Charlotte hoped they didn't belong to her mother. Unfortunately, the precise rhythm of her steps did seem to indicate the presence of her mother, though given that there was a larger than normal gathering of people, it stood to reason that her mother's gait would be rather less unique than normal.

"I can see your slippers, dear," her mother said. "I know you're behind that curtain."

"How very curious," Lady Isla murmured.

"What an odd location for you to stand," her mother continued.

"Are you Mrs. Butterworth?" the duke asked.

"Oh, yes, I am," her mother said gaily.

Ice shot through Charlotte, and she hurried from the comfort of the curtain. She blinked into the bright light. Flames on tall candles, the white wax adorned with crystal holders, glimmered, magnified by mirrors, dancing before her.

She wished the flames would not move.

She wished the face of her mother would not look nearly so startled.

Charlotte was afraid to look at the other faces.

She wasn't going to permit the duke to tarnish her mother's evening. She was still functioning. She hadn't succumbed to her illness yet. She wanted to be in charge of deciding how her life should be lived, and it didn't involve seeing her parents' and sister's despair, and it didn't involve her sister giving up her hope for finding a husband and steadying their family's finances.

"Oh, there you are, Charlotte." Her mother composed herself and beamed. "It would have been most embarrassing if I was speaking to someone else's slippers."

"Sneaking behind the curtains? How terribly quaint." Lady Isla laughed, and Charlotte moved her gaze in the direction of the voice. The woman was not difficult to find; everyone seemed to be staring at her in open adoration.

She was beautiful.

Charlotte didn't use that word lightly, even in her mind, but the fact remained unmistakable.

The woman moved toward her, obviously not beset by clumsiness or some other affliction. Emeralds glimmered from her throat. The jewels were popular with some of the older women, but this woman did not seem to be using them for their throat wrinkle disguise purposes. Her skin appeared smooth and dewy. The waistline of Lady Isla's gown was lower, in the very newest style, bestowing her with a doll-like appearance men most likely adored. Even her slippers were jeweled, and they sparkled against the black and white tile of the floor.

Charlotte stiffened. Her pale pink dress seemed unsophisticated. One never spent long observing a single pale-colored flower.

Lady Isla continued to assess her, though she'd lifted one brow. Charlotte had the distinct impression she was the reason.

The woman narrowed the distance between them. "Your hair is messy, my dear. That curtain could not have been good for it."

Charlotte reached toward her hair, but the woman tilted her head, and her eyes glimmered ice. "Oh, dear. That is your normal updo."

Charlotte felt like a three-year old who'd wandered into the wrong wading pool, to discover not only was she in the wrong location, but she couldn't even swim.

"Why were you hiding there?" The duke's eyes rounded. "Did you feel faint? Perhaps the dance was too much exertion for your health..."

She jerked her head toward her mother. "I-it was quieter."

"Who wants quiet at a ball?" Lady Isla asked.

Charlotte was silent, and she twisted her handkerchief together.

"Let me introduce you to the baronet's son," Mama said. "He's *most* important."

Lady Isla widened her eyes. Mama hadn't recognized the duke.

"Oh, you should hurry then," Lady Isla said, her lips twisting imperiously again. "It must be so *special* when people who lead quiet country lives attend a ball. I can't imagine how dull their lives must otherwise be."

Charlotte's chest hurt, and she allowed Mama to drag her toward the baronet's son. They moved across the ballroom floor.

"Where did that man go?" Mama mused.

"I met Sir Seymour," Charlotte said.

"Well, you can't marry him," Mama said. "He's already got a wife." She peered about the ballroom.

Charlotte looked about the ballroom, half-expecting to see a squat man in attire that wouldn't look amiss in a hunting field, with hair with rather less gray than Sir Seymour's.

When Mama squealed and pointed, the man in question, though he was squat, didn't appear like he'd been anywhere near a hunting field. He wore a mauve waistcoat of such vibrancy it gleamed even from his distant location. His blond hair was carefully coiffed, and he was surrounded by a bevy of elegant gentleman.

"He appears occupied," Charlotte said.

Mama sighed. "He does, doesn't he?"

"Charlotte!" Georgiana squealed, and Charlotte turned her head to see her sister and father approaching. "You were dancing! With the duke!"

Mama's eyes rounded. "Truly?"

"Indeed," Charlotte said.

"Why how ever did you manage that?" Mama asked.

"He asked me."

"Darling, I cannot believe you danced with a duke." Mama fanned herself. "How marvelous! I wish I had seen it. It would have been the most incredible thing."

"Apart from your daily visions of me." Papa smiled at Mama.

Delicate pink spread across Mama's face, and she giggled in a manner that made it very easy to imagine what they would have been like in their youths.

Mama and Papa seemed so happy now. How could Charlotte tell them she was going to die? She didn't want to cause them anguish. Would her last days be of hearing them wail and despair?

She couldn't permit the duke to share her secret. She'd have to convey the importance to him at once.

"Was that the man near the curtains?" Mama asked. "He was most handsome."

Charlotte smiled. For once, Mama was absolutely correct.

"Though I did wonder why he was inquiring about your health," Mama continued. "He did seem most concerned."

"He was?" Georgiana frowned, and her eyes glimmered with intelligence.

Mama blinked. "I suppose that was odd. It is not an eccentricity commonly attributed to dukes."

"Oh?" Charlotte tried to laugh, and Georgiana's eyes narrowed.

Hopefully the duke doesn't tell anyone of my condition.

Chapter Eight

CHARLOTTE HAD TO STOP the duke from informing anyone of her illness.

The thought stayed in her mind during the rest of the ball, and it remained in her mind on the carriage ride home and as Flora helped her prepare for bed. It even remained in her mind as she lay in her bed, willing herself to sleep.

I need to speak with him.

The thought was ridiculous. Everyone would talk if she visited him at Hades' Lair. Gaming hells were no place for women. The *ton* frequented such clubs, and her presence would be noticed straight away.

I could visit him at night—

She shook her head, willing herself to not ponder the possibility of simply calling on the duke now. That was the sort of thing everyone would think inappropriate, even though the streets would be quiet, and she would have less chance of discovery. After all, when she wore her black hooded cloak, she would blend perfectly well.

In fact, it would even be logical to visit him now.

If it would be improper to visit him at any time, why not visit him when fewer people would be around to see him?

And though London was dangerous, this neighborhood was not the East End.

Anyone who saw her might think her a servant or shopkeeper's wife.

There'd be no reason for them to assume she was someone who frequented *ton* events.

It was all utterly logical.

Charlotte had always been termed good. She was definitely not the sort of person who was expected to visit dukes at odd hours of the night. But perhaps she'd been termed good simply for her tendency of not speaking with the frequency of Georgiana. By the time she was born, Georgiana had been contentedly babbling away, most likely about the virtues of flowers and plants, while Charlotte's language did not yet extend to more complex statements than "Mama" and "Papa." So Georgiana became the talkative one, and Charlotte became the quiet one. And because being talkative was only a virtue for French salon proprietresses, Charlotte was also referred to as good. Her blond hair made it easy for members of her father's congregation to compare her to an angel. But Charlotte didn't want to only be good. She wanted...more.++

She lifted her torso and pushed her blanket away. Leaving this house would be tricky. It would be difficult to explain to anyone why she was wandering it. Hopefully everyone would be sleeping, but if not...

She calculated the likelihood of detection.

If only her room faced the street. Georgiana's room had a tree beneath it. Unfortunately, Charlotte's room faced a courtyard, which while quiet, would not help her get to the duke's club. The large door downstairs was heavy, and she would almost certainly wake someone up if she closed it.

Perhaps she should use the roof. There must be an advantage to it not having a sharp tilt, and it wasn't rain protection. Flora had told her before that the roof leaked. No doubt Flora would be happy when the season ended and they all returned to Norfolk. The maid had certainly given enough hints, musing over the loveliness of the landscape. Flora preferred writing letters to her family in France on her half days than exploring the capital.

Papa would be happy to know at least one person considered that county with great favor.

She sighed. She should be content to return home. Norfolk wasn't unpleasant, even if it was small and far from London. The long stretches of flat land allowed one to see for miles, and there was something about the open expanse of landscape that she craved. But somehow seeing the ocean before her, even though it was miles away, and not in comfortable walking distance, had made her one day long to actually sail on it, actually visit new destinations.

Lady Isla was right. Perhaps she had lived a dull, countryside life.

But one thing Charlotte was certain of: she was dying, and it didn't matter if she misbehaved.

She attempted to put on her darkest dress, the one she'd worn in mourning for her grandparents. The clasps were difficult to hook in the dark without Flora to assist her. She decided to just slip on her dark hooded cloak over her shift. At least she managed to put on her boots by herself.

Now is the time.

Her heart tightened again, but she pushed the door open.

The corridor was dark, and her parents' snores made their presence on the other side of the corridor impossible to forget. Her heart soared toward her throat, and she fought the urge to slink back to her bedroom.

I can do this.

She wavered at the staircase. She wouldn't call the staircase grand, but its bannister curved in an interesting manner and it landed in the foyer. From there it was only a few short steps to the main doorway. Hopefully no one would wake up when she opened the main door.

But the door is noisy.

She shouldn't risk it.

She hesitated and then opened the door to the servants' staircase. She'd never gone down it before, even though her family had come to London for the past three years. There was no bannister, and she moved her hand to locate the wall. She found it quickly—the staircase was narrow. The room smelled musty, and she hoped her fingers were not becoming dirty. She didn't like it when her fingers became dirty.

Finally, she came to the end of the staircase and pushed through a new door. The floor beneath her changed to an uneven tile, and she took care to avoid stepping too heavily. She shouldn't be able to see the tile, and she frowned. Light glowed from beneath a door.

Candlelight? At this hour?

One of the servants must be awake. Would Cook start so early? She didn't think so, but... Charlotte pressed her lips together and quieted her steps.

The servants' door was at the end of this corridor. She wouldn't have far to go. She just needed—

The door from the lit room creaked and swung open.

Flora stood before her. "Miss Charlotte?"

Even though she was forever being told she was too thin and too short, invisibility was something she was evidently nowhere near achieving. "It's me."

"What are you doing?" Flora's French accent seemed to have vanished momentarily.

Her family's maid might not be as intimidating as traditional guards. Flora clutched some paper in her hand, and some ink stained her fingers. Charlotte was quite certain her maid possessed no sword or pistol to direct at her, but that did not make her presence any more appealing.

Flora might do her hair and help her dress, and she might know how uncomfortable Charlotte found certain textures and how loud noises distressed her, but despite their closeness, that didn't mean that the maid wouldn't scream.

"I-I thought I might go on a walk," Charlotte said.

"At this hour?" Skepticism sounded in Flora's voice. "You shouldn't be here, *mademoiselle*," Flora said, her French accent restored, and Charlotte's shoulders sank.

"Please don't tell anyone," Charlotte said.

"Are you meeting someone?" Flora asked.

Charlotte was silent.

Meeting was most certainly the wrong word.

"Are you in trouble, mademoiselle?"

"Me?" Charlotte shook her head vehemently. She resisted the urge to give a hearty laugh, the forced shock peculiar to those who'd tasked themselves with lying.

The night might be dark, but Charlotte felt Flora's gaze remain on her.

"I'm going to pay a call on someone," Charlotte said matter-of-factly.

"It's past midnight."

"It's important."

And it's the sort of call one couldn't make in the daylight.

In the daylight, anyone could see her.

And in the dark—

"Well, I'm going," Charlotte said.

Flora pressed her lips together. For a horrible moment, Charlotte thought she might scream to wake up the house, but she only said, "I'm coming with you."

"You don't need to," Charlotte whispered.

"I'm worried about you," Flora admitted. "And I understand being put in bad positions, *mademoiselle*."

"It must have been difficult to come here during the wars," Charlotte said. "Being French."

"Er—yes," Flora said.

Charlotte opened the servant's door to the outside. They were at a lower level, and she climbed the stairs to the street.

"Now where are we going?" Flora whispered.

"To see the Duke of Vernon."

The maid gasped. "Oh, I do need to tell your parents, mademoiselle."

"Nonsense. I simply need to discuss some matters with him."

"You mean you're not attempting to—"

"To what?"

"Bed him?" Flora squeaked.

"Good heavens, Flora. That would be quite out of the question. Wherever would you get such a thought?"

"I've—er—heard he's handsome."

"Well that has absolutely nothing to do why I'm seeing him," Charlotte said primly.

Chapter Nine

FLOORBOARDS CREAKED outside his office, and Callum frowned. London had not been unnaturally warm. This whole year had been chilly. There was no reason for the floor to be expanding, as if revolting from the shock of heat. Had he been at Montgomery Castle, he would have dismissed the noise as belonging to a particularly adventurous dog, undaunted by the darkness, in pursuit of crumbs and exploration. But Callum did not have a dog in London, even though it occurred to him that this should perhaps be rectified.

The noise halted.

Perhaps Callum was experiencing an overactive imagination, the sort normally derived from delighting in penny dreadfuls or magic lantern performances on windy nights. Perhaps townhouses in the middle of London were susceptible to ghosts, even though he would have thought if they truly existed that he'd be more likely to find them either in Montgomery Castle or Lord McIntyre's estate in Scotland.

He forced himself to concentrate on his ledger. The numbers were not adding up. There was a mistake.

He attempted not to become distracted by thoughts of Miss Charlotte Butterfield. Her impending death shouldn't concern him.

Death befell everyone. His parents were dead. His guardians were dead. Many of his friends were dead, victims of Bonaparte's army. The exact destinations of the Frenchmen's swords and muskets had varied, but too many encounters had been fatal.

No, Callum should not be pondering the fate of Miss Charlotte Butterworth.

And yet Callum's heart still squeezed at the injustice of her illness.

The elegant townhouses in Mayfair offered an illusion, aided by an abundance of columns and porticos, that life was perfect. One only had to wander from the neighborhoods' boundaries or venture downstairs to where the servants toiled, to see that was not the case.

The tick-tock of the grandfather clock in his bedroom seemed less an expression of Schwabian technical expertise than a harbinger of doom, the sort of morose item that had no place in any room, much less a bedroom.

Tick. Tock. Tick. Tock. Tick. Tock.

Callum didn't wait for the pendulum to complete its gloomy task. He strolled to the clock, opened the glass case, and paused it. The ticking stopped. If only he could pause Miss Charlotte Butterworth's march toward death with similar ease.

Footsteps moved over the corridor, and Callum frowned. Most likely, it was a servant, even if servants shouldn't be wandering the corridors at night. Heavens knew they did more than enough work during the day.

Still.

That was *definitely* the sound of footsteps.

And there *definitely* should not be the sound of footsteps here.

Could someone be robbing him? Ice prickled his skin, and Callum opened his desk drawer. He grabbed a knife from inside.

The door opened, and a woman appeared.

He blinked, and she strolled into the room. The woman had blond hair and a face he could never forget.

"Miss Butterworth?" he asked.

"Your Grace." She curtsied, as if she were calling on him, as if there could be a normal reason for her presence. White fabric seemed to glow from the hem of her black cloak. White fabric that looked curiously like a shift. White fabric that made him conjure up all sorts of indecent images. Plain cotton shouldn't be that enticing, and he groaned.

"What are you doing?" he asked.

"Visiting you. I think it is obvious."

"There's nothing obvious about you coming here." He glanced at her again, wondering if he'd conjured the white fabric. He had not. Her cloak was slightly open, perhaps from the movement of her curtsy, and the strip of pale fabric seemed to move enticingly. That blasted shift was what she wore to bed, and images of Miss Charlotte Butterworth on a bed seemed dangerous. He averted his eyes. "How did you get in?"

"Hat pins have many uses. I've always found their main function rather uninteresting."

He had a strange urge to chuckle. "I'm certain you are aware of how utterly inappropriate it is for you to be here."

"We are not alone," Miss Charlotte Butterworth said briskly. "I brought my maid."

"Your maid?" Surprise jolted through him.

"I hadn't planned it," she admitted. "But you can consider her a chaperone."

Personally, Callum thought a maid was more likely to be a false witness to a compromise. Charlotte couldn't be concocting such a scheme? He hadn't thought her the type.

He ran a finger along his cravat, wishing he'd not decided to loosen it at some point tonight.

He knew he shouldn't be relieved Miss Charlotte Butterworth hadn't taken it into her mind to compromise him, and yet... Speaking with her was pleasant, and he'd had a sudden vision of not just speaking with her.

Her figure was petite and perfect.

Blast it, this was his fault for not seeking a mistress. There were more than sufficient married women and eager opera singers who could have been happy to bed him. He shouldn't be looking at fresh-faced debutantes with imperfect hair, no matter how late at night they appeared in his room.

"Flora!" Miss Charlotte Butterworth said. "Please introduce yourself to the duke."

After a pause, a dark-haired woman stepped from behind an oversized vase. "*Oui, mademoiselle.*"

Callum would have to remember that his library did not require hiding places, especially when the people hiding were strangers.

He turned to the quivering woman. "I take it you are Miss Charlotte Butterworth's maid?"

The woman nodded and dipped into a deep curtsy. "Indeed, Your Grace."

"You may rise. No point in being uncomfortable when it's already so late."

"*Merci*, Your Grace."

Callum frowned. Something about her seemed almost...familiar, and he narrowed her eyes. She looked away hurriedly.

Most likely, she'd worked at another establishment he'd attended. Maids might not switch employers often, but they did it with more frequency than their employers switched homes.

Or perhaps he'd seen her at the park.

That's it.

He returned his attention to Miss Charlotte Butterworth. The woman was certainly worth his attention. "Why exactly are you here?"

The woman did not seem the type to desire to steal from him, but one could never be certain. Vicar's daughters could hardly be considered wealthy, and perhaps she believed she attended church with sufficient frequency so as to avoid the fiery flames painted in ominous Dutch artwork even if she did resort to blithely breaking a commandment.

"I thought it unlikely that I would be allowed entry in the daytime."

He chuckled. "You are correct."

"So I had to come." She shrugged. "I thought it unlikely you would call on me."

"Well. You were correct in that." He realized too late that the statement could be construed as ungentlemanly. Blast it, did she think because he asked her to dance that there would be a romance between them? Perhaps this was the reason men advocated staying away from debutantes.

If Miss Charlotte Butterworth was insulted, she did not reveal it. "I will be brief. You asked me if there was anything you could do. Because of my health." The last word was said almost in a whisper, and she glanced in the direction of her maid.

Oh.

It was far nicer not to dwell on her impending death. She seemed livelier than the other women in the *ton.* Her words were more surprising, as if she'd not worked them out beforehand at an elite finishing school.

"Yes," he said. "I'm happy to help. In any way."

Even though he'd recently met her, he realized with surprise that he meant it.

She raised her chin, as if seeking to summon the courage to speak.

"I have some connections in Bath," he said. "If you would like, I might be able to arrange for your family to live in a townhouse there."

Her eyes widened, and her mouth dropped open. "You would do that for me?"

He rubbed his hand on the back of his neck. "It wouldn't be that difficult. Many people are in London for the season." *And heaven knows Hades' Lair has clients eager to impress me.*

"It's very kind," she said seriously. "But not what I had in mind. I-I was hoping you would keep my illness quiet."

"I can understand your family will want privacy."

She averted her gaze.

Damnation. The chit still hadn't told them. Was she meaning to do so? "You must tell them."

She shifted her feet. "I-I will. But in the meantime, I want you to promise *not* to tell them. I don't want you to tell *anyone.*"

"You should tell them, and then you should go to Bath."

"I don't intend to spend the last months of my life with my family fussing over me and sitting in water with people who have infectious diseases."

The maid gasped, but Miss Butterworth raised her chin and widened her stance.

Brave chit.

"I know people say it's healthy to do that," Miss Butterworth said, "but scientifically, it seems questionable. I want my sister to have a nice season. My illness would disturb it, making it even more difficult for finding a husband."

"She could find a husband next year."

Miss Butterworth shook her head. "You don't understand. She's on her third season, and the expenses are already too large. Please." Her voice wobbled. "Let me keep this secret for longer. It's my request."

Well.

He couldn't very well go against a dying woman's wishes.

And yet... How could he condone her not telling other people who cared about her? Other people who might fight for her? Or who might want to spend more time with her?

I would have desired to spend time with my parents and with Aunt Edwina.

"If there's a chance your life might be prolonged, you should do everything to prolong it," Callum said.

"Perhaps you're correct. But I want to decide if they know. Because why give up the rest of my comfort and disrupt my family's chances of landing a husband for my sister, for only a chance? Especially when that chance is small, and when I would most likely be forced to go to Bath, to be surrounded by new people, forced to bathe in water with people in similar circumstances in pursuit of a cure that might not happen. I take pride in my research ability, and I know Dr. Hutton is the very best."

Something about her rigid back made his heart ache.

He pressed his lips together. He hated that she was dying. He'd grown accustomed to seeing the numbers of his parents' generation dwindle and to see fewer familiar gray-headed people at balls and on the fields. He'd even grown accustomed to seeing his school friends disappear; war had a habit of doing that. But once a person managed to reach adulthood, Callum rather expected to see them for a few more years.

Miss Charlotte Butterworth wasn't fighting Frenchmen, she wasn't toiling in a field, she wasn't living on some horrible street in London—she shouldn't be able to be taken away.

Dr. Hutton was renowned. Even Callum knew that. People traveled vast distances to see him. If the man was convinced Miss Charlotte Butterworth's condition was helpless, it must be.

"Why risk coming here when someone could see you? Your reputation might be ruined."

"I was willing to risk that. Taking appropriate precautions—dressing in black, taking my maid, lowered my risk. Besides, soon I'll be dead."

He rose and tried to act matter-of-factly, even though her words seemed to squeeze his heart. "Let me have my groom prepare a carriage for you and your maid for your return."

"Percentagewise, the likelihood of anything horrible happening is very slim."

"Any percentage would be too high for me," he declared, and rang the bell. He soon gave instructions to a surprised looking servant.

"I refuse to go yet," she said.

Tension surged between them, and she dropped her gaze to his ledger. "Are you having difficulty?"

He blinked, not expecting the change in conversation. "Accounting is most difficult."

"Perhaps." She was silent for a moment, but her face soon transformed. "I wager I can balance your sheets."

He smiled. "That is kind of you. But accounting is quite complex."

"You're probably right. But if I can find the mistake in your ledger, will you keep your mouth shut?"

"I suppose I could—"

"Very well." She approached him. "Now please stand up. I find accounting is most successful when not viewing ledgers upside down."

He blinked. "Do you do much accounting?"

"I manage my father's personal accounts. And the vicarage's."

It was impossible to not note the pride in her voice.

Most women did not come and announce an affinity for accounting, and most fathers did not task their daughters with such work. The chit couldn't be older than eighteen. She had the dewy look about her of a debutante. It was the sort of look he generally avoided.

Everyone knew one didn't go about entering into relationships with such waifs, since they were quite likely to take the end of such relationships seriously. After all, they'd been raised to assign crocheting and other impossibly dull tasks with seriousness.

He should be demanding she leave the room, but he couldn't deny the hopeful gaze in her eyes. He sighed. "Very well. If you can solve my ledger, I will honor your wish."

I'd already decided to.

Miss Charlotte Butterworth settled into the chair.

"Now what are you trying to do?" Miss Charlotte Butterworth asked. "These accounts are decades old."

Callum flushed.

"And this gaming hell was only installed much more recently," Miss Charlotte Butterworth continued.

"What seems to be the problem?" she asked.

"There's too much money," he said.

"Most people wouldn't think that a problem."

Her eyebrows rose, and his cheeks flushed.

"Only a duke would consider that a problem," she said.

"I know." The warmth of his cheeks increased.

"Well," she said. "You may as well tell me. I won't be around for so long."

Callum winced.

He shouldn't be sharing his ledger with anyone. And this was the old earl's ledger that he'd taken from Wolfe's shelves.

*Still...*It would be nice to tell someone. He'd never told anyone before.

And Miss Butterworth... She wasn't in his circle. He doubted she would gossip about him, but even if she did—he doubted she would be believed. Perhaps if he were musing about something else except his parents, the thought she would not be believed might upset him, but now it only imbued her with the quality of safety.

"My parents died when I was seven," he said.

Her eyes widened. "I'm so sorry. That's young. It must have been—"

"Horrible. I know. It was." He sighed. "My guardian always told me my parents had died penniless. He took over their debt."

"That was kind of him."

"Indeed." Callum gave a tight smile.

Everyone was always telling him how kind Lord McIntyre had been.

"But I'm not seeing any expenditure that would relate to paying off that debt. I'm worried Montgomery Castle might have fallen further in debt." He tried to keep his voice calm, but it seemed to quiver with anger.

Lord McIntyre had told him he was paying his parents' debts. Had that never been done after all?

"Then you should hope the interest rate is low," Miss Butterworth said matter-of-factly.

"I know," he said, settling into a chair beside her. "It just does not make sense. Lord McIntyre always insisted I marry his daughter."

"Lady Isla?"

He nodded.

A frown came over Miss Butterworth's face, and he wasn't certain what he should ascribe it to. Probably it was Lady Isla's behavior at the ball.

"I'm sorry she was rude to you," he said. "She often is."

Miss Butterworth rifled through the papers, not answering him.

He sat back in his seat, unaccustomed to this.

After a while, she took off her cloak, and he swallowed hard. She was, indeed, wearing only a shift. The fabric was far too thin. He could see exactly the curve of her bosom, exactly the shape of her figure, ponder exactly—

"Is something she wrong?" she asked.

"N-no," he stammered and forced his mind to muse over more appropriate things.

"I find comfort essential in problem solving," Miss Butterworth declared. "More would be done if more people were not distracted by their attire."

An hour must have passed, but she did not remove her focus from his books. Her concentration was impressive.

"Ah ha," she said finally.

"What is it?"

"Lord McIntyre did not pay off the debt of your parents' castle."

"That odious man. I suspected it, but—"

"He did not pay it off, because there was no debt."

Callum blinked. "That's impossible."

"Did you ever receive notification from a debtor?"

He shook his head.

"Look," she said. "Here are regular payments. The increase each month is by the same percentage, down to two decimal marks. Too precise to be a coincidence."

"So he was getting money... That can't be unusual."

She gave him a hard stare. "He was pretending the estate was in debt. He was reaping the rewards."

Callum furrowed his brow.

There must be a mistake.

But his heart hurt. This wasn't a mistake, he was certain.

"Of course, this is not sufficient proof. And there might be another explanation. But the vastness of the sums does make it seem highly likely that money from your father's estate was coming into your guardian's account. I would suggest you investigate further."

Callum had been so foolish.

Lord McIntyre had hurt him even more than he'd suspected at the time.

He should have realized that long ago. The property was not mortgaged. It had never been mortgaged. That was something the neighbor had told two little boys who didn't know any better, and there had been no one else, no family members—not after his aunt had died—who had said something, and no official who had thought to inform him.

His fingers tightened.

Perhaps Lord McIntyre had paid off his father's former steward, the one man who would have known. Or perhaps the steward had simply never heard the lie. Stewards didn't run in the same circle as aristocrats, no matter if they were really the ones who ran the estates and secured the aristocrats' continued good fortune.

He'd always thought his parents had squandered their money. It had seemed odd after all. Why would they have? Had they really held too many parties?

He hadn't seen signs of great expenditures, but that didn't mean they hadn't existed.

He'd been so foolish for so long. He had known better than to trust Lord McIntyre, but about this, he hadn't thought to question him.

But then, as a child, he hadn't even known basic financial terms.

He'd been told his parents left him with no money, and that Lord McIntyre was rescuing him, out of a kind-hearted neighborly instinct that Lord McIntyre never failed to remind him of.

"Was he a close relative?" Miss Butterworth asked softly, pulling him from his reverie.

Callum's feet felt unsteady. "He was no relative at all. Just a neighbor."

"Well, I can't imagine your relatives didn't protest."

"My parents came from small families," he said. "My mother had a sister. I-I think, now, she most likely did suspect something. But she died a few months after my parents."

"I'm sorry, Your Grace," she said.

"It was a long time ago."

"That doesn't make it better," she said, and he nodded.

"I want revenge."

"Then don't marry Lady Isla," she said.

His eyes widened. "What would you do?"

She shrugged. "You can marry anyone. Why not someone inappropriate?"

His lips twitched, and for a moment, he imagined putting a ring on the finger of a scullery maid or a lady of the night.

The servant knocked on the door. "The carriage is ready, Your Grace."

"Ah." Callum and Miss Butterworth rose and he made sure the driver had instructions to take her straight to her home and nowhere else.

"You will keep your promise?" Miss Butterworth asked sternly.

"Indeed. I always would have," he confessed.

She flushed, as if realizing the impropriety of her visit.

He watched her depart, conscious that he should feel relieved, but feeling oddly disappointed. He returned to his study and stared at the accounts.

Lord McIntyre had swept Callum and Hamish away, perhaps thrusting some forged papers in some official's direction, perhaps not, since what official would question the word of a prominent earl? The old earl had spent his life telling Callum and Hamish that he'd rescued them both from certain poverty, and that the only way they could pay him back would be if Callum one day married Lady Isla.

Callum snorted. He wasn't going to marry her.

Not when the matchmaker had killed his aunt.

Not when the matchmaker had lied to Callum his entire life, making Callum feel so guilty.

No, this was when Callum would become a man. He would take the money, and then he would be certain Lady Isla never married him.

He would marry someone else.

It didn't matter whom he would marry. The more inappropriate, the better. A thought occurred to him, and a smile played on his lips.

Chapter Ten

CHARLOTTE TOOK ANOTHER slice of bread. Her appetite hadn't vanished with the doctor's death notice. Perhaps appetite loss would come later. Dying was a most novel experience. She rubbed her eyes, still sleepy from the night before.

Mama barreled into the morning room, and the laces on her cap fluttered, waving in such different directions, one would have thought she was conducting an experiment in physics.

"You have a gentleman caller," Mama shrieked.

Charlotte must have misheard.

"You must get ready, my dear child," Mama said. "He's in the drawing room. Waiting for you."

"Oh." Charlotte scrambled up.

"You must look your best. And you really don't today."

Heat rose along Charlotte's neck. "Is there really someone right outside the door?"

"Precisely," Mama said gaily. "First gentleman caller you've ever had."

"Who is he? Did you take his name?"

"Name?" Mama scoffed. "You think we've procured a butler? No, I ran out to tell you, since I know you needed to look nicer than you do."

"Oh," Charlotte whispered.

"Why on earth are you whispering, dear girl? Is something wrong with your throat?"

Charlotte didn't answer the question, but Mama became preoccupied with fussing over Charlotte's hair, even though Flora had just done Charlotte's hair today. Mama's best efforts seemed only to be dismantling Charlotte's curled locks, since Mama's fingers could hardly be described as curling tongs, no matter Charlotte's own fondness for her mother.

"But, Mama," Charlotte said quickly, "if he is right outside this door, he can probably hear everything you're saying."

"Oh? I'm not one for chemistry."

"Physics," Charlotte said. "You're not one for physics."

Mama beamed. "I had no idea you were so impressed by my chemistry skills."

Charlotte sighed. The education of women did not include very much. The cracks on the door did seem of the wide variety, and she had the dreadful feeling the sound could make its way from room to room with little hindrance.

It's probably not the duke.

Why would the duke call?

Had he decided to tell her parents after all? If not of her fatal illness than of her visit last night? Her visit was the sort of mad thing one would do in the middle of the night when one's reputation seemed in tatters, and it was most certainly not the sort of thing one did when it was no longer three in the morning and one's life seemed rather more normal, rather more like it always did.

Perhaps if she were truly lucky, Mama had simply fabricated the man. Papa was always saying Mama's imagination was far too strong, and perhaps he had in fact had a point all these years, and she had been in the habit of conjuring up whole men who just happened to have the pleasing sort of facial features that only the Duke of Vernon managed to have.

The room did seem silent.

That had to be a good thing, though the duke was likely far more educated than her and might not make a whole lot of noise, especially when all by himself.

"Is Papa in the drawing room?"

"Oh, he's in there, too," Mama said gleefully.

"But I don't hear him speaking," Charlotte said.

She hoped it was because the door was rather thicker than she'd thought, despite the large cracks in the frame, but if Papa was there, well Papa had a tendency to—

"He's reading, dear. It's as if you don't even know him," Mama said.

This was mortifying.

If a family like hers was fortunate enough to have a duke call, the duke was certain to think the family might possess sufficient curiosity, not to speak of courtesy, to converse with him. One was not bound to think a family very educated, if they spent their time musing over whatever reflections some Grecian had scribbled down years ago, before even the concept of dukes had even been invented and people in England were considered barbarians and were busy running one another over with chariots.

She unwound herself from Mama's clasp.

She had to see for herself.

"My dear, you must wait!" Mama shrieked.

Charlotte pushed the door open, and her heart tumbled to the floor.

Papa and the duke were sitting inside the parlor. The duke rose instantly, and Papa lifted his head from the book. "My dear child."

Opposite him was the duke.

All six foot four inches of him. She hadn't measured his height previously, but since the ceiling was only six feet two inches, and the man seemed hunched in an angle to which he'd not previously been prone, she suspected his height extended another two inches.

Whomever had designed the room had likely never suspected a man of such aristocratic proportions would be inside.

But it was unmistakable.

She would recognize the duke's curly blond locks anywhere, as well as his high cheekbones and bright blue eyes that seemed to radiate amusement.

Oh, dear.

He was amused.

That was not good.

Well, perhaps it was better for him to feel amusement than another emotion—anger, disapproval. Certainly, there were many emotions he could feel, and perhaps amusement was a good one for him to have selected, but she didn't quite like that the duke had entered her home and had seemed to have begun by laughing at it, if only in his eyes.

"Well, if you're going to stand at the door, you may as well come back here so I can finish your hair," Mama said.

Charlotte's cheeks warmed, and the duke's eyebrows seemed to have reached a higher perch.

"You have a visitor?" Georgiana asked, brushing past Mama.

"Oh, she does," Mama said. "And he's most handsome."

The duke's lips turned up, and Charlotte swallowed hard. Fire burned through her, and she curtsied quickly.

The duke bowed deeply, with a flourish to which Charlotte was not accustomed.

Georgiana peeked her head over Charlotte's shoulder, and then gasped.

Charlotte glanced at Georgiana. Georgiana's eyes widened, and she seemed to even somewhat quiver, even though Georgiana was decidedly not the quivering type.

Georgiana had been a debutante two years ago and had been attending balls ever since.

She would recognize the duke. Oh yes, she knew who was in the room, and she knew how utterly unlikely it was that he was there.

Papa might imagine his girls were merrily dancing at balls, but he didn't know that was far from the truth. They were lucky when some of their favorite wallflower friends were in attendance at the balls.

"Well, let's all go in," Mama said, giving Georgiana and Charlotte a slight push.

"Your Grace?" Georgiana stammered.

"Miss Butterworth," the duke said smoothly. "It's a pleasure to meet you."

Georgiana gave a wide-eyed look to Charlotte. She was probably wondering why no one else was speaking.

Charlotte knew English.

She had been taught.

In fact she'd read many books written entirely in English, but right now she wasn't certain if she'd ever learned an approximation of the order in which words were supposed to be spoken.

Unfortunately, spewing words without any context was unideal in making her be comprehended.

The duke's eyes still twinkled, though he did look a bit uncertain.

"Your Grace?" Mama asked behind her.

"Mrs. Butterworth," the duke said again, bowing.

"Mama, may I present the Duke of Vernon," Charlotte said.

Mama blinked.

"Is it a nickname?" Papa said casually, flipping through his Plato. Papa was most attached to it.

"No," Georgiana said.

Papa jumped to his feet, and his book toppled to the floor and gave a mighty echo. The quality of the vellum should not be in any question. "If you are a duke, what are you doing here?"

"Well, obviously the dear boy must know my relatives," Mama said. "Now please, have a seat, Your Grace."

The duke settled into the chair opposite Papa.

He was handsome, far more handsome than anyone had the right to be, as if he'd stolen the handsomeness from other people. Could there be enough beauty left in the world for others?

Her mother's shoulders relaxed, and Charlotte tried to summon a similar sense of calm.

Surely the duke won't mention my visit?

Anxiety rushed through her.

Charlotte's heart beat far too quickly, and her cheeks continued to heat. This shouldn't affect her like this.

"My dear daughter has made this," Mama said quickly, perhaps sensing Charlotte's embarrassment, and pointed at some embroidery.

The embroidery was horrid. Why exactly anyone would want to use needles to pierce fabric and malign it with bright thread in various shapes had always been beyond Charlotte.

"How delightful," the duke said, with such enthusiasm that he soon entered into a conversation with her mother on her own embroidery skills. "Do you embroider as well?"

Mama beamed. "I do!"

"You must show me your work," the duke said, glancing at Charlotte.

"You find it interesting?"

"Most," he said.

Mama shoved some embroideries of flowers in his face, and he expressed admiration for each one.

"You know all the years I've lived," the duke said, "I've never done any embroidery. It seems most complex."

"I've been doing it since I was a little girl," Mama said, still beaming with obvious pride.

Charlotte smiled. It was nice to see her parents so entertained.

"You're reading Plato," the duke remarked to Papa.

"Oh, indeed," Papa said. "Are you an admirer?"

"How could I not be?" the duke asked, obviously assessing from the great many books on the philosopher of a safe answer.

"Now who is your favorite continental philosopher?" Papa asked.

"They all have their admirable traits."

Papa frowned and shook his head. "Oh, that won't do. That won't do at all. They're all different, you see. And the differences are most important."

"The differences make each philosophy more unique."

Papa tilted his head. "Oh, I suppose that's true. Good point."

Charlotte found her breath becoming more even as the attention moved from her.

Flora brought in some tea, avoiding the duke's gaze. Charlotte was happy for something with which to distract herself.

"To what do we owe the pleasure of your visit?" Mama asked the duke.

"I came to call on your younger daughter," the duke said.

"You danced together," Mama said. "It's the blond hair." Mama pointed to Charlotte's hair proudly. "My eldest daughter is quite lovely, but she has red hair. Much more difficult to marry off."

"Perhaps I'll become an old maid," Georgiana said.

"I'm sure you'll have proposals," the duke said awkwardly.

"And yet she has no prospects," Mama said.

"Well, I didn't meet your eldest daughter. Perhaps if I'd met her things would be different," the duke said in an effort of perhaps politeness. "I mean, perhaps I did see her at balls—"

"Yes, that hair color is quite distinctive," Mama sighed. "It really is a shame we're not in the last century anymore. Then we could just slap a wig on her, pat her face with chalk, and no one would be the least bit wiser that her hair is red and her nose is speckled with freckles."

"I believe speckled is not quite the right word," Papa said. "Speckled implies a minute amount of freckles when—"

"In my case there is a lot," Georgiana said, rolling her eyes to the heavens. "I know. Believe me, I know."

"So you just met my dear daughter yesterday and you are already calling on her," Mama said, with a pleased expression on her face.

"Quite."

There was an awkward silence. Though Mama had often mused aloud about what might happen when one of her daughters received a gentleman caller, with the exception of a curate who was fond of calling on Georgiana, though everyone suspected that his presence was mostly because of Cook's superb sweet-making abilities, the fact was that until now, gentleman callers had always been rather abstract, like one of the mathematics problems in the sort of books women were not supposed to read.

"Well, I suppose now is as good a time as any." The duke patted his purse. "Busy night at the club."

Charlotte stiffened. Papa was unlikely to condone the fact the duke was involved in running a gaming hell, but since Papa stayed far away from the gossip broadsheets and Plato was unlikely to have foretold the duke's not-so-wonderful business habits, Charlotte supposed that the duke was safe from being preached to.

Well.

The duke cleared his throat and patted his purse again, and a strange flush rippled through Charlotte's body.

It's not possible.

And yet, he had come here. That was odd.

It's not that, Charlotte thought. *It can't be that. It certainly can't be—*

"Oh, my Lord!" Mama shrieked. "He's kneeling."

The duke *was* kneeling.

He was kneeling on the floor before Charlotte. Mama clapped her hands. "It's happening. Oh, my dear! It's happening. Where are my smelling salts? My dear Mr. Butterworth, I must get my smelling salts!"

Mama sprang up, even though sudden movement seemed to indicate Mama didn't seem in danger of fainting. "My dear! Perhaps I should ring for a servant. Flora? Flora?"

Flora poked her head into the room. "Madam?"

Papa stretched his arm toward Mama and placed a hand on her leg. "My dear Mrs. Butterworth—"

"Be quiet," Mama said.

"I only meant," Papa said, "that you should perhaps let the duke finish."

"In truth, he hasn't even started," Georgiana said.

"You are not helping," Papa said sternly. He turned to the duke. "Now, my dear boy, what were you saying?"

"Probably nothing," Charlotte said quickly. "He probably lost something. A handkerchief perhaps." She looked down on the floor and left her chair. "Perhaps I should help him—"

"No, no." Mama moved across the room, hauled Charlotte up and set her back into her seat.

Mama seemed quite athletic today.

"I only wanted to say," the duke said. "Will you, Miss Charlotte Butter—er—"

"Worth!" Mama said brightly. "It's Butterworth."

The duke nodded and he seemed even more pleased. He hadn't seemed to mind her parents' multiple breaches of etiquette, and Charlotte narrowed her eyes. Most men did not seem pleased at the ridiculous sound of her last name, but it seemed to cause the duke to veritably beam.

"Will you do me the honor of being my wife?"

"Of course she will," Mama said enthusiastically, clapping her hands together. "My dear, I am so happy to have witnessed this lovely proposal."

"It was quite standard," Georgiana said.

Mama glared at her. "It was the most romantic thing that I had ever heard."

"More romantic than Papa's proposal?" Georgiana asked.

Charlotte gasped. She couldn't marry anyone. Not with a doctor's death sentence. She couldn't be a wife, even though that was the very thing she had been raised to be. She could never be the hostess of her own townhouse, she could never have her flower arrangements dot her own carefully chosen furniture, and she could never embroider her children's clothes.

But mostly, she would never live long enough to have children and secure her husband's heir.

She would miss the scent of flowers in the springtime, miss the sight of sunrises splattering rosy light over the landscape, miss the simple joy of sipping good tea. But marriage—the one thing she'd always longed for, would be an impossibility. One couldn't marry a man and die six months later. Not on purpose.

Chapter Eleven

SHE'S NOT GOING TO accept.

Miss Butterworth's eyes were decidedly dry. They managed to even appear...angry. At least, the manner in which they bored into him seemed decidedly unromantic. Her body seemed rigid. Wasn't a woman of her position supposed to swoon?

His ancestral home might be in Scotland, a fact that might wrongly give some women the impression of a lifetime condemned to consume haggis and endure perpetual precipitation, but that didn't change the fact he was a duke, and her lineage was decidedly less impressive.

What if she refuses me?

He shuddered.

He didn't want to consider the scandal of proposing to someone who rejected his advances. This whole endeavor had been to tarnish the McIntyre reputation. His goal had not been to tarnish his own.

"I'm gaining a son!" Mrs. Butterworth shrieked, and with a happy sigh, Callum realized it didn't matter what Miss Charlotte Butterworth might say—her mother considered the proposal accepted.

"Indeed you are," he said amiably, before Miss Charlotte Butterworth might interject with any unfestive statements.

Her face darkened, and he decided it would be more enjoyable to direct his attention to his new relatives rather than his new betrothed.

"When I saw you last night, I did not realize we would be spending every Christmas and Easter together for the rest of our lives," Mrs. Butterworth said.

"His Grace has not extended an invitation," said his new betrothed's sister.

Mrs. Butterworth waved her hand in an impatient gesture. "It is implied." Then her face grew more solemn. "I do hope they burn Yule logs in Scotland. That is quite the nicest thing about Christmas." She directed her attention to him. "Tell me, Your Grace. Are you a Yule-log burning enthusiast?"

"I'm sure I could be," Callum said.

Mrs. Butterworth's eyes widened. "You mean you don't know?"

"I've never given it much thought." He paused, trying to remember if he'd experienced a Yule log before, but then shook his head. "My parents died when I was seven, and my guardians—" He winced at the word. "—expressed a fear that placing a burning log in the house might lead to the manor house burning down."

"Such nonsense," Mrs. Butterworth said. "We will come for Christmas, and we will have a Yule log. Or dearest Charlotte and you can come to the vicarage in Norfolk."

He might have proposed, but that did not mean he intended to make uncomfortable journeys across the country to stay in likely dreary vicarages. Norfolk was infamous for its general provincialism. Most English aristocrats favored the area that stretched from Hampshire to Kent, and provided them occasional glimpses of sloping verdant fields and blue water. Some Northern aristocrats prided themselves on the rugged landscape in which they found themselves, though Callum suspected they delighted less in the steepness of the slopes and the picturesque qualities rendered than by the ample supply of coal mines underneath that same rugged landscape and the equally ample supply of workers whom they could force to toil there. No one though seemed to give much thought to Norfolk. It was generally seen as too flat and a destination for the lesser classes in the East End.

"Please forgive my mother," Miss Charlotte Butterworth said. "She is enthusiastic. I'm certain His Grace has spoken too quickly."

"I did not," he said.

"Of course he didn't, my dear. Men don't wander into people's homes and accidentally propose. When they do it, they do it with intention. Now you two must kiss."

"Kiss?" Callum said weakly.

"You're engaged." Mrs. Butterworth beamed.

"The man is a gentleman," Mr. Butterworth said. "He does not need to kiss anyone."

"The man is a duke," Mrs. Butterworth said. "No gentleman at all."

"I-I." Callum glanced at Miss Butterworth.

Kissing her had not been part of the plan. Proposing to her had not even been part of Miss Charlotte Butterworth's plan, and he shifted his legs. The thin worn carpet was not a proper barrier from the floorboards, and they groaned beneath him, like a whistle to signal distress.

Perhaps he shouldn't have proposed. Her pale face when he'd first hinted at the possibility had not differed greatly from most people's reactions when he spoke to them. One woman had even swooned when he'd asked her to dance, and he'd taken Miss Butterworth's silence as a surprise that would soon lead solely to pleasure.

Perhaps he'd miscalculated. Perhaps, despite all the ways a union between them made sense, she did not see the benefits.

"Of course I accept," Miss Charlotte Butterworth said finally. "But a kiss is unnecessary."

"Oh, I suppose you have a lifetime for that," Mrs. Butterworth said, sinking back into her pillows, and a sadness appeared in Miss Butterworth's eyes.

I'm going to kiss her.

Callum narrowed the short distance between them and clasped her face in his hands. Her cheeks were softer than velvet, and the shade of her blue eyes exceeded any color that the sea might conjure.

"You needn't," she said.

"I want to," he said, realizing it was true.

In the next moment, his lips brushed against hers.

He'd experienced many first kisses with women before. He'd kissed women on balconies, ballroom music wafting to them and stars above them; he'd kissed women in rose gardens, inhaling the floral scent carefully cultivated by expert gardeners, and he'd kissed women in palatial bedrooms, over the finest imported sheets. None of his prior kisses had involved crouching near a too small chair in a sparsely decorated parlor, before a bevy of the woman's relatives.

The kiss shouldn't cause him any delight, and certainly no heart swelling, and yet a thrill of something very like excitement cascaded through him, and when his lips touched hers, he was unwilling to let go, delighting in their soft succulence.

"How romantic," Mrs. Butterworth pronounced, fluttering her hands. "How very splendid."

Much as he welcomed a positive reaction, the only reaction he cared about was Miss Butterworth's, and he gazed at her. Her eyes had a glazed look to them.

"Are you quite well?" he asked quickly. Perhaps kissing was not recommended. He shouldn't have forgotten her frailty. The doctor had said she should experience no excitement. He broke the distance between them. "Your eyes appear dilated, and your cheeks are flushed."

"Are they?" Miss Butterworth pushed her hand to her cheeks, as if to tell the temperature, but Callum added a dry throat to his list. Her voice had seemed most normal only two minutes before.

This is not good.

He didn't want to damage her health.

"I suppose I should go," Callum said abruptly. "Enough excitement."

"I'll see you to the door," Miss Butterworth said, springing up in a manner that did not necessarily convey her impending invalid state.

They rounded the corner.

"What are you doing?" Miss Butterworth demanded.

"I thought it was obvious."

"You just proposed," she wailed.

"Indeed."

"My parents think we're going to marry!"

"We are."

She narrowed her eyes. "But why—? You don't know me—"

"My dear Miss Butterworth," he said airily. "Or should I call you Charlotte now?"

"Call me anything you like. Just explain it to me."

"You gave me the idea. Last night."

She peered around her, and her face whitened. "You mustn't mention my visit."

He shrugged. "I won't. Not that it would matter. We *are* getting married."

"But why? You know I can't give you what traditional wives can—"

"I know," he said gently. "But you gave me the idea."

"Me!" Her eyes widened, and then she blinked. "You mean… I'm someone inappropriate."

He frowned. He didn't like hearing those words on her tongue.

"Because of my parents. My mother's too talkative, and my father is too scholarly, isn't that correct?"

The room seemed to have become warmer.

"And we don't have any money, and I'm not a Lady Charlotte. I'm just a Miss Butterworth."

"Soon you will be a Your Grace," he promised. "Soon you will be a duchess."

"Is this because you feel sorry for me?" she asked.

He averted his eyes. He did feel sorry for her. She was dying. He wouldn't be much of a person if he didn't feel the slightest twinge of sorrow.

"Perhaps," he admitted, and she stiffened. He despised himself for causing her distress. "But that doesn't mean I would marry just anyone who was sick."

"Well, that's discerning of you."

"I mean—I like spending time with you," he said, realizing that it was true.

And that kiss—

He could desire more than spending time with her. He shook his head.

"Obviously you cannot have any excitement," he said. "Obviously we wouldn't have a traditional marriage." The words felt false in his mouth, and he wondered if perhaps there was not really so very much obvious about the statement. "But that doesn't mean I can't marry you, if you'll have me."

"I can't give you an heir," she said.

"Fortunately I have a twin brother filled with responsibility." He frowned. *Hamish better not learn of the wedding.* "Besides, given your situation—"

"You'll remarry," she said. "After I die. And *that* woman will give you an heir."

"Er—precisely," he said, not desiring to meet her eyes.

"In that case, I accept," she said.

"Good," he said, conscious of a strange relief flooding his body. It shouldn't matter. It was easy for him to find anyone to marry, much more someone inappropriate. But marrying someone other than her felt wrong.

Besides, forever wouldn't be very long. If they despised each other, and he didn't think they would, it wouldn't matter. In the meantime, he could do his best to make her last months as pleasant as possible. He would make sure she was cared for. He would be a dutiful husband.

"I'll call on you tomorrow," he said.

"Oh?"

"I believe it's appropriate," he said. "Now that you will be my bride. I've heard a June wedding is considered ideal."

"Then June it is," she said softly, and he beamed.

Happiness flitted through him, and he told himself it was just because he had gotten his way, and he liked getting his way. He strolled back to Hades' Lair.

If Wolfe hadn't left to travel, he would shock him now. Now surprising him when he returned would have to suffice. He had the odd impression that he would not mind calling on her.

Chapter Twelve

RAIN PATTERED AGAINST the window panel of Callum's breakfast room, and the net curtains on the windows did not disguise the gloomy gun-metal sky. Rain had fallen incessantly over the past few weeks, not ceasing when St. George's was booked, the banns were posted, or when a new suit was ordered from the tailor. Hyde Park emptied, as the unremitting rain halted even the most consistent visitors from making their daily strolls.

Footsteps sounded, and his brother appeared. Callum forced himself to smile, wishing the poor weather had hindered Hamish's arrival last night from Scotland. Any hope his brother was a mirage Callum had conjured in a nightmare vanished. No mirage could glower with such force.

Hamish wasn't supposed to be here. Callum hadn't invited him.

The fewer people who knew about the wedding in advance, the fewer chances someone would convince Callum not to go through with it. Thankfully, Wolfe had remained away, and Lady Isla had left London. The people he did tell were sufficiently shocked. Charlotte had been scarcely groomed to be the wife of a baronet's son, much less a duchess.

Unfortunately, Mrs. Butterworth, in her enthusiasm, *had* invited him, and Hamish's sudden presence was unmistakable.

The mirrors in the foyer reflected Hamish's never ceasing glower.

"You shouldn't marry that chit," Hamish growled. "You're betrothed to someone else. Have you forgotten?"

"Naturally not," Callum said. "But I desire to marry Miss Butterworth."

Hamish gave him a hard stare. Sometimes Callum wondered if Hamish had always looked at him with such open abhorrence, or if it had started after they'd moved into Lord McIntyre's home. The old earl had always been quick to criticize Callum.

"I hope you do not intend to stop the wedding," Callum said.

Hamish didn't respond. *Blast* it, Hamish should respond. Ice swept over Callum, as if he were tumbling down some Norwegian mountain in the midst of winter.

"Lord McIntyre took us in," Hamish said. "How could you break his heart?"

"Our late guardian no longer has a heart to break."

Hamish winced, and Callum instantly felt guilty. Any urge to tell Hamish more lessened. Hamish had adored the late earl. Could he tarnish their former guardian's reputation?

At least Callum had the benefit of spending time with Mr. and Mrs. Butterworth. Hamish, on the other hand, only had memories of their late guardian and his wife, and his brother seemed determined to forever color his mind with the most enthusiastic version of the events. Callum supposed that the old earl had been fond of Hamish, and had helped him develop an interest in Scottish architecture.

"And what are Miss Butterworth's motivations in desiring to marry you?" Hamish continued, moving to a new attack.

"Besides my general attractive appearance?" Callum joked.

Hamish scowled, and Callum bit back his grin. Callum shouldn't jest. His brother apparently never jested.

"You're a duke," Hamish said. "You should be careful. You can tell me, if you've been placed in a compromising situation. Is she blackmailing you?"

"What on earth would she have to blackmail me about?"

"You run a gaming hell. Perhaps you've done something to warrant blackmailing."

Callum sighed. The gaming hell had been a method to get revenge on the old earl. When the war was happening, Callum had been occupied with defending Britain, but its completion signified he'd return to defend his family's honor.

Wolfe was happy to have Callum's name to attach to the gaming hell, and Callum was happy to have access to Wolfe's vast collection of papers. Now that Charlotte had given her theory after examining the late earl's ledgers, Callum only had to prove it.

"You are humiliating Lady Isla," Hamish said sternly.

"Do you think so?" Callum remembered her behavior to Charlotte at Sir Seymour's ball and he feared his lips might be ascending upward despite his best efforts.

Hamish fixed a level gaze on him. "You've been irresponsible."

Callum stiffened. His brother had it all wrong.

Blackmail.

As if Charlotte were capable of such a thing.

As if Charlotte would have the least idea what to blackmail him about.

Callum's indiscretions did not extend to blackmailable offenses, and if they did, nice daughters of vicars would not be the ones to carry it out.

In truth, Callum should have asked her to dance immediately, when he'd first seen her at a ball, no matter the supposed state of his engagement to Lady Isla.

Perhaps he should tell Hamish more after all.

Would he believe me?

Callum's stomach hurt. Some questions might have unpleasant answers.

Before Callum could decide whether or not to confide in him after all, the butler announced the carriage was prepared, and they exited the breakfast room.

"You don't have to come with me to visit the Butterworth family," Callum told his brother.

"I wouldn't want to miss meeting your betrothed." Hamish climbed into the carriage. "I—er—wonder what she looks like."

"Then you'll find out," Callum said.

"Are we going to Kensington?" Hamish pondered. "I wonder where she lives."

"The edge of Mayfair," Callum said.

"I'm learning so much," Hamish said.

Something was off in the man's naivety. Hamish liked to pride himself on knowing things, even when he didn't at all, but in this respect, he seemed to differ.

How odd.

Callum resisted the temptation to dwell on the whims of his brother's arrogance.

Finally, the carriage pulled up at the Butterworth's London townhouse.

Hamish scrutinized the narrow building. "It's quite small."

"She only has a sister."

"Family size has nothing to do with it," Hamish said.

Callum agreed, silently.

Most people in the *ton* seemed quite happy to put their family in grand townhouses that stretched over multiple floors whether or not they had the children to fill the rooms.

Callum and Hamish disembarked from the carriage and stepped into the small house. The maid, Flora, flushed when she saw them and hurried them into the drawing room. Mrs. Butterworth had transformed the family's drawing room. Flowers and herbs lay on every surface, and nobody seemed to mind the competing scents that wafted through the room.

"What horror is this?" Hamish glanced warily about the room.

"No horror," Callum said, "and remarkably close to happiness."

Chapter Thirteen

THE WEDDING HAD ARRIVED, and butterflies had taken residence in Charlotte's diaphragm. They fluttered up and down, sending tremors through the rest of her body.

Marrying a duke. Marrying *anyone.*

It was the sort of thing any other debutante would have declared an impossibility. And yet, the day was here. Charlotte was in her finest dress even though it was only the morning.

She'd never considered herself sentimental and she was hardly going to begin now. She did her best to ignore the manner in which light shimmered over the columns of St. George's. Georgiana's alternating sparkling eyes and worried eyes.

"You don't have to marry him," Georgiana whispered. "If you don't care for him..."

Charlotte smiled. Georgiana was romantic.

Whatever the duke's faults, and proposing to her in front of her family was one of them, he was a good man. He'd treated her kindly, almost tenderly, calling on her every day before the wedding. The only problem with the wedding was that she might forget this was a transaction. He needed an unsuitable bride, and she was one.

He hadn't even invited any guests. His brother was here, but that was on her mother's invitation, and he'd been horrified at his brother's sudden appearance. It seemed evident that she was doing her part at being an inappropriate bride; he didn't even want anyone to see them marry. Oh, well. He'd be able to shock the *ton* when it was over. Despite their mother's habit of telling everyone about the wedding, Charlotte was under the impression that most people did not believe her. A woman like Charlotte was not supposed to marry a duke.

When she approached St. George's, the door to the church was locked. Georgiana attempted to open it, but no one was inside. Charlotte shifted her slippered feet under the portico, conscious of the befuddled passers-by who were unaccustomed to seeing people in bridal attire stand in front of church doors.

Her chest tightened. Surely, the duke hadn't meant this to be a jest? She shook her head. He was too kind. She couldn't believe it of him. But perhaps his brother had somehow convinced him not to marry her? Flora had packed her trousseau. She was expecting to move into his townhouse this afternoon. She was not expecting to go back to her family in disgrace. That was certainly not how she desired to spend the last months of her life.

Papa approached her. "I'm afraid no one is inside. It seems the wedding is off."

"My poor child," Mama wailed and put her hand on her chest in a melodramatic gesture. "Woe is me."

The normally jovial faces of her parents lacked any joviality. In fact, their countenances seemed most distressed. They stood stiffly in their formal attire.

Wheels ground over the cobblestones, and she recognized the duke's carriage.

He'll know what to do.

BLAST.

The church was shut, and the Butterworth family was distraught.

Callum glanced at Hamish. His brother wasn't precisely smiling, but his lips were contorting into an odd position as if he were struggling to control them. A dull red blush spread upward from his neck when he saw Miss Georgiana Butterworth. At another time, Callum might have thought his brother was taken by her, but no doubt guilt was the impetus for Hamish's uncharacteristic unease.

"How dreadful that the minister has vanished," Hamish said to the Butterworth family, but his brother was no good actor. Callum could tell the man was pleased. "I'll try to help you find the minister."

Mr. Butterworth nodded. "I would be most grateful."

The two left in Mr. Butterworth's carriage, but Callum held no hopes that they would be successful. If he knew his brother, Hamish had bribed the minister and had ensured no one else would marry them, most likely dropping the names Lord McIntyre and Lady Isla to convince them of a moral onus. The clergy seemed most susceptible to entreaties to righteousness.

Miss Butterworth's sister approached Callum as soon as her father and his brother rounded the corner. "I must speak with you."

"Very well."

"I fear your brother is intent on stopping the wedding. H-he believed me to be your betrothed and climbed into my room with a large bribe."

Callum's eyebrows jolted up. "Indeed?"

Was Hamish bribing everyone?

"I-I said no of course," Miss Georgiana Butterworth assured him. "I would not like to come between my sister and the man she loves."

Loves.

Charlotte's family was under the impression that he was madly in love with Charlotte and she with him. Charlotte and he could hardly tell them that they were marrying because he found her family inappropriate. What would it be like, though, if he was marrying someone who truly adored him?

He forced himself not to contemplate that, instead considering his brother's interference.

Callum had failed Charlotte.

It had been Callum's idea for them to marry, but he hadn't even managed to secure the ceremony. He'd allowed Charlotte's mother to spend her time creating elaborate floral and herb arrangements for the wedding, and yet no wedding had taken place.

This was a disaster.

Fury at his brother coursed through him. His brother was supposed to be defending him, and not the offspring of their former guardian. Hamish seemed determined to stop the wedding, spurred by a false sense of heroism no doubt derived from reading too much Walter Scott. People in Scotland seemed to have developed the belief they were more heroic than others, simply for what their ancestors might or might not have experienced in past centuries.

His heart raced, and his formal attire felt too stiff against his skin. "I am sorry my brother behaved so abominably."

Not that it mattered. His brother might believe he'd stopped the wedding, but he'd only postponed it. Nothing was going to compel Callum to give up the wedding. He would not allow Charlotte to spend her last months as a woman whose engagement had fallen through. He needed to convince Hamish that he'd been persuaded not to marry Charlotte after all, and then Callum would marry her quickly.

He thanked Miss Georgiana Butterworth and pulled Charlotte aside. "I am afraid there will be no wedding today."

"Oh."

Callum didn't need to excel at observation to note the wobble in her voice, and his heart tightened. Perhaps she was worried that the wedding wouldn't take place after all. Increased fury pummeled his veins. "We will still marry, of course."

"G-good. Shall we try again next week?"

Marrying another time would be logical.

"We probably wouldn't be able to book St. George's," he said.

"That's fine," she said. "After all, this is a very small wedding."

Her words made him cringe. He wished he'd done a larger wedding, one where it mattered more if something occurred to it. Charlotte shouldn't feel her wedding was a minor event. No wedding should feel like that.

A thought occurred to him. *Elopement.*

Nothing was more romantic than an elopement. Elopement involved travel and inconvenience. No one would think a wedding small if it involved an elopement. No one would muse that he had allocated meager resources to a wedding if they'd eloped.

Mrs. Butterworth's elaborate bouquets would wilt were they to postpone the wedding a few days, and he didn't trust Hamish to not manage to stop the next wedding.

They had to convince Hamish the wedding was off...for good. And that did not involve rushing about London, booking another church and having Mrs. Butterworth commence the creation of new bouquets.

Perhaps Charlotte would scoff at the idea. There were hundreds of reasons why an elopement was unideal.

"What would you say to eloping?" he asked.

Charlotte's eyes widened. "That would be most exciting."

"In a good manner?" he asked tentatively. It was important it be in a good manner.

"I've never thought I would elope," she said. "Vicars daughters tend to marry in churches."

"We can still marry in a church," he said.

"Not a blacksmith's shop?" Her eyes glimmered, and even though their wedding had been canceled, and even though he'd never been more upset at his brother than now, he found himself smiling back.

"Have you been to the Channel Islands?"

She blinked. "No. I haven't been outside of Britain."

"The Channel Islands are part of Britain." Callum frowned. "Somewhat. Beautiful beaches, stunning sunsets, and more importantly, the—"

"—1754 Hardwicke Act doesn't apply," Charlotte said, and her voice was somewhat breathless.

He smiled. The woman had a habit of finishing his sentences, and he, of hers.

Perhaps it wasn't a real marriage, with no expectation for lifetime companionship and children. Even the most unhappily men and women in the *ton* seemed to expect their spouses to make appearances at their side at balls, even if they stayed at opposite ends. Charlotte's body would be under the ground by the end of the year, but something caused him to think perhaps their marriage *could* have been real.

"Consider it a sunnier Scotland." He stepped closer to her. "Now, what do you say? Because it you desire it, we should leave soon. Before my brother returns."

"I accept," she said.

"Good." He found himself beaming. He should be grateful at the opportunity to not marry at once. Didn't men mourn their freedom after they married? "Let's talk to your mother and sister."

The conversation was quick. Charlotte's older sister promised to do everything to keep Callum's brother from following, and Callum told her to offer his brother the use of Callum's carriage to return to Scotland. Then Callum led Charlotte down the steps of St. George's, conscious of onlookers. They were used to scattering people at weddings with flower petals. Witnessing people in fine attire ascend the steps of the church and then make mournful exclamations, must be rather more novel.

"Follow me." Callum flagged down a hack, and the driver pulled toward him abruptly.

"That won't take us far."

He smiled. "Perhaps not. But it will take us to Hades' Lair where I will grab some funds, and from there we can go to the Thames and then to Guernsey." Ideally, he would return to his townhouse, but he did not want to meet Hamish. He thought Hamish would return to St. George's, but he could not be certain. Fortunately, he always kept some things at Hades' Lair.

"I will need to go to my parents' home to get some items from my trousseau. One does not go to Guernsey and back in a day."

"No, one does not."

I'M ELOPING.

Excitement and nervousness competed inside Charlotte. Charlotte wasn't the type to elope, but everything had changed since she'd met the duke.

Riding in a carriage with him would be the first time they'd been confined together without anyone else. Even when she'd crept into his residence, she'd been well aware Flora had been with her. She wasn't certain whispered conversations in corridors counted. As she became aware of his presence, she was certain it did not.

The man towered over her, a fact clear now he was not perched awkwardly in a chair that had once belonged to her Great Aunt, clasping a teacup in his hand, which had been how she'd grown accustomed to seeing him.

He gave the driver instructions and then assisted Charlotte up the short metal stairs before he settled into the seat opposite.

Callum's mouth tightened, and Charlotte despised the worry in his gaze. A man like this wasn't supposed to worry. He was a duke. He was supposed to drink brandy and play cards. He was supposed to ride his curricle through Hyde Park without worrying about the wellbeing of the women he saw. The most burdensome work he was supposed to do was posing for the occasional portrait, an exercise in stillness that would have caused the athlete in him to rebel, even though everyone who saw it would marvel at the softness of his velvet tailcoat and the pleasant symmetry of his features.

Finally the hack moved, bumping over the cobblestones, and she tried to ignore the man's scent of fresh linen that wafted over her, his long legs that almost touched hers, and his chiseled face.

It suddenly seemed very important that Flora come with her to Guernsey.

"I'm sorry my brother ruined the wedding," Callum said. "I—"

"—Didn't even invite him," Charlotte finished. "It's not your fault. Besides, Mama seemed quite pleased with the idea of an elopement. Rather more romantic than even dining on a wedding breakfast."

Callum smiled. "I'm glad."

Lady Isla had been cruel when she met Charlotte, assuming, correctly, that Charlotte never ventured beyond Norfolk and London. Charlotte wanted to have some adventure. She wanted to be on a ship, to feel waves beneath her and to smell salty air. Most of the world was ocean, and it seemed wrong to exit the world without experiencing something of it.

Once the hack stopped before her parents' townhouse, Charlotte rushed out. The door swung open.

"Your Grace." Flora curtsied deeply. "I trust the wedding was pleasant?"

Charlotte gave a tight smile. "There's been a change of plans. We're eloping."

Flora's eyes widened. "Your father does not approve after all?"

"He approves, but my betrothed's brother does not."

"I see." Flora fixed an assessing look on her.

"We wanted to get my trunks. Since I won't be staying here already. If they're packed of course," Charlotte said, finding herself stammering. She'd never done an elopement before and the process was novel.

"*Naturellment*," Flora said. "They are already packed. I'll have Samuel bring them to the duke's carriage."

Charlotte's cheeks warmed again. "As a matter of fact, we are taking a hack."

Flora blinked. "A *hack?*"

"Not far," Charlotte hastened to say.

Flora nodded, but Charlotte had the impression she did not truly understand. After all, the duke was in possession of multiple carriages, and should not require to take the plainest one available to anyone with coin.

"I know it's an unnatural mode of transport," Charlotte continued, "but it is vital that the duke's brother not follow us, and the duke loaned his carriage to his brother."

"How clever."

"Besides," Charlotte continued. "We are simply going to the Thames."

"You're taking a ship?"

Charlotte nodded, and this time she smiled, contemplated again being on a ship. She'd only ever been on a rowboat before in the local pond, and she suspected it did not count as a representation of all water transport. "Indeed. We're going to the Channel Islands."

"How wonderful," Flora said.

"Will you come with me?" Charlotte asked.

"To Guernsey?"

"There will be many French people," Charlotte said. "You'll adore it."

Flora's face paled. "I-I can't go."

"But Flora... You were going to move with me to the duke's."

"And I am happy to do so. In Britain."

"Why is that?"

For a moment, Flora hesitated. Finally, she sighed. "I-I am scared of boats."

"Oh."

"They can be quite dangerous," Flora said. "The water is...unpredictable."

"People have been crossing the English channel for centuries."

"Not everyone with success," Flora said.

"I suppose that's true."

"I wish I could come. But I can't."

"Because of your fear?"

"Er—yes," Flora said. "Forgive me."

She shut the door, and Charlotte was left to stare at the wooden frame.

"What is the matter?" Callum asked.

"Nothing," Charlotte said, forcing herself to sound cheerful as a servant carried some of her trunks into the hack. "I'd just hoped my maid would join us."

"I'm sorry," Callum said. "Of course, if you would prefer to stay after all..."

Charlotte considered the possibility. "Is that your preference?"

"I am always up for adventure," he said.

She smiled.

She knew what London was like.

She didn't know what the rest of the world was like.

If she was going to die soon, she wanted to experience something of the world.

She wanted to see the ocean...up close.

She wanted to stand on a ship.

She wanted to visit a place where people spoke a different language.

"I'm up for it," she said.

"Magnificent," Callum said. "Then let's hurry."

Right.

Goodness knew how long her mother would keep quiet. Her mother didn't tend to keep secrets.

Callum took her hand, and excitement thrummed through her. They hurried toward the hack.

The uncharacteristically blue sky had vanished, replaced with thick steel-gray clouds. Callum's blond hair no longer gleamed, no longer glowed, but the austere surroundings did not hamper his appearance.

Charlotte swallowed hard.

She climbed into the hack. The light was dim, even though the curtains had been pushed all the way open, and she glanced at the modest street.

She squared her shoulders. Her parents had pinned all their hopes on having one of their daughters marry well. She was pleased she'd been able to fulfil their wishes.

She'd come so far, and she wasn't going to halt now, simply because her maid was too scared to go on the ship with her. The notion would be ridiculous, and she gave a wry smile. At least she knew the duke was not interested in marrying her for her figure. He could bed any woman he wanted without the hassle of an uncomfortable hack journey and a most likely even more uncomfortable ship voyage.

No.

She was safe with him.

Their agreement was not based on something as flimsy as desire.

She climbed into the coach, and the hack driver headed toward Hades' Lair.

"I'll only be a moment," Callum promised her when the coach stopped.

"Remember to fetch Lord McIntyre's old accounts."

His eyes widened. "But this is to be your holiday."

"It is important," she said.

"Thank you," he said solemnly before leaving.

He soon returned, and the coach continued to the Thames. The rain pattered against the roof of the carriage.

"We should be out of Mayfair now. I'll open the drapes." Callum stretched toward the window, and Charlotte averted her eyes. The action was senseless, for she still glimpsed his broad chest and the manner in which the fabric tightened against interesting parts of his torso. His blond hair shifted and fell over his brow, masking his eyes. Rustling sounded, but the light in the carriage hardly shifted. She turned toward the window. The slate gray sky offered no joy. Condensation clouded the window, and Callum swept it away with his gloved hand. The view remained smeared, but gray row houses, stained from smoke, were visible. Their drab exteriors nearly blended with the ominous sky.

This wasn't Norfolk. No sturdy oaks and chestnut trees stretched lofty branches into the sky over which squirrels raced. No sheep grazed in picturesque pastures, and no lambs ventured into spontaneous hopping competitions. No cows ran through verdant grass, moving their speckled coats elegantly.

This is an adventure.

Chapter Fourteen

THE HACK JOSTLED OVER cobblestones. It crept over the streets, and despite the hack driver's occasional shouts, the journey took longer than in Callum's ducal coach. Men pushing wheelbarrows and servants rushing about doing errands didn't halt for a hack.

Changing his mind about the prudence of the elopement would no doubt be sensible. Yet when the hack stopped before the ship to Guernsey, his doubts disappeared. He clasped Charlotte's hand, noticing her soft exclamation of surprise, helped her over the irritatingly narrow steps of the hack and toward the ship.

The ship to Guernsey was not the most magnificent in the Thames. That honor belonged to the ships heading to the Americas with their bevy of finely attired passengers. But he ushered Charlotte through the crowd of sailors and toward the wooden gangway. Birds darted before them and skimmed their legs into the water. They squawked merrily, unafraid of the water, before they swept back into the air.

Dockworkers moved methodically, arranging wooden crates in neat piles and hollering instructions to any newcomers with absolute confidence. Their blue and white attire did not match the Thames's perpetual murky waters, but it reminded him of the azure waters and diamond crested waves that they might later encounter.

If Charlotte wanted adventure, he would give it to her.

He grabbed her hand, even though they weren't technically married yet, and even though he was most assuredly breaking protocol. *Never mind.* They'd be spending more than one night on the ship before they landed in Guernsey.

Boats and ships packed the Thames. The river shouldn't have felt narrow, but it seemed as if all the world had attempted to be crammed into the river. Shore boats left triangular ripples in the water.

Beside him, Charlotte stiffened, and her legs swayed, even though the ship barely moved.

"Is your heart well?" Callum asked quickly.

"It feels fine."

"You seem ill at ease."

Charlotte's smile wobbled. "Sometimes places feel too crowded to me, even though everyone else manages. It's silly."

"It's not silly," Callum said. "I'll have the steward show us to our cabin. I think you'll feel better when we've left the Thames."

Charlotte nodded, and Callum hailed a steward.

"I am the Duke of Vernon, and I will be traveling to Guernsey with this lady."

The steward's eyes widened and then he bowed deeply. "Your Grace. We are so honored that you have chosen our ship on which to travel. I will give you the best room we have."

"This lady requires a private cabin," Callum announced.

"A private one?" The steward's expression faltered. "I'm afraid, Your Grace, that that might be impossible. At this late notice..."

Callum frowned. Charlotte was not going to be sharing the room with various servants making the passage. His future wife deserved the very best.

"There is a woman of some importance on the ship," the steward said hesitantly. "She is the sister of the Baron von Braunschweig. Perhaps she would be amenable to sharing her room. It is quite pleasant."

Callum sighed. If the baron's sister was anything like the baron, she would be an unideal companion. The baron's vainness was well known. *Still.* It would have to do. "Please arrange it."

The steward nodded and scurried away.

Callum took Charlotte's hand and led her to a seat. "Tell me, what are your symptoms?"

"Symptoms?" she squeaked. "My heart hurts sometimes."

He nodded gravely. "Is there something that brings on those spells? I want to know," he said.

"But you're not a doctor."

"No. But I don't want to see you suffer."

She tilted her head. "I-I suppose. I don't like touching."

He released her hand.

"I mean—that was fine," she admitted. "Almost nice. But I like to know in advance, if that makes sense. If I can see you, before you touch me, that helps."

"Oh."

He didn't know anyone who didn't like touching.

Touching was a very good thing.

"Sort of like how milkmaids have to approach cows. Only from the left side."

His lips twitched.

"You're laughing at me."

"Smiling," he protested. "Not laughing."

Her shoulders slumped down.

"It's fine," he said gently. "I've never had a woman compare herself to livestock before."

A pleasant rose color bloomed across her cheeks.

"I understand though. So no sudden touching. What else affects you?"

"No strong smells," she said.

He raised his eyebrows. "Some of the men at balls smell quite strong."

"You're laughing again."

"I'm in perfect agreement."

"The cologne... It's too much."

"No cologne then." He frowned. "How do I smell?"

"Most delicious," she said quickly, and then blushed. Her eyes were bright, and her cheeks rosy. The woman was beautiful, even if she did not seem to be the least bit aware.

"What happens if someone touches you?"

"It feels horrible."

"I hope no one hurt you," he growled.

What could cause her discomfort with...touching. Everyone liked being touched, didn't they? That's why even the briefest of touches in dancing was scandalous. That's why waltzing had been banned from Almack's for so long. Because humans craved being touched and even the slightest touches might lead to other things.

"Give me their names," he said. "I'm a duke. I can—"

"Do things?" Her eyes widened. "No. Nothing happened."

"Oh," he said, trying to not simmer.

"Forgive me," she said. "It's just you're quite different from what I expected."

"Are you saying I have a bad reputation?"

"The very worst," she said, and then a tawny rose ascended her cheeks again. "I'm sorry. That's probably not an appropriate thing to say."

Normally he wouldn't mind that he had a bad reputation.

Normally he would even take pride in it. A bad reputation meant he wasn't living up to the expectations of his late guardians.

But now... Now he despised his reputation.

"What else makes you uncomfortable?" he asked.

"Loud noises. It hurts my ears. More I think than it hurts other people's ears. It gives me headaches."

"Then I'll avoid them," he said.

"You must think me so silly." Her face was still pink, and something in his heart panged.

"Not at all. Prevention is a good remedy."

"I know it's not like this for other people. I'm difficult."

He contemplated the other ladies of the *ton*. Charlotte had never once spoken poorly of anyone, and she'd talked of numbers with more passion than most ladies could muster if placed in Vauxhall or a fine haberdashery.

Charlotte didn't even share a room with her sister, and he was not going to have her start now. People who were shy seemed to benefit from having space. It was not something he craved, but his brother Hamish had always seemed to take great pleasure in occasional solitude.

Charlotte could take his cabin, and he could room with Lord Braunschweig. He could tolerate a few uncomfortable nights if it lessened Charlotte's anxiety.

"You'll have a private cabin on the ship. The finest here."

"Doesn't that belong to you?" she asked.

"I can room with someone else."

"I wouldn't want you to do that," she said.

"Nonsense," he said. "It's my pleasure. I want you to be comfortable here. Besides, I can room with the German baron"

Charlotte smiled.

"What is it?" he asked.

"You're just not quite what I expected."

"And why is that?"

"You're a duke who owns a gaming hell," she reminded him. "You're not supposed to be sensitive."

"I'm a man of many facets," he said easily. "I know what it is to be uncomfortable."

"I doubt that."

"I do," he said.

A few passengers observed them.

And then the ship moved and made its way through the crowded river.

It shouldn't have been unexpected. They'd traveled here expressly to sail. And yet...

Callum had never expected to cross the channel again. When the White Cliffs of Dover had shone like a beacon as his ship had sailed toward Kent, filled with soldiers, he'd thought he could never leave the shore of Britain again.

And yet here he was, blithely heading across.

Charlotte looked divine. Her blond hair was swept back, but curled tendrils framed her face, not quite covered by her lace veil. The thin lace didn't mask her features, rather it only served to make her appear more heavenly.

Heavenly.

The word was not one he'd anticipated ascribing to her. Heavenly was a word men who made love matches might use. Everyone knew Charlotte was a bluestocking. She wasn't known for her charms, and yet Callum had an urge to take her into his arms.

Heaven.

It was a location to which she would soon be visiting.

Perhaps that explained his sudden sentimentality.

CHARLOTTE HAD PLANNED to be installed in the duke's townhouse, awkwardly arranging menus with his housekeeper and trying to look authoritative before a bevy of London servants who would be aware of just how unexpected her position as duchess was. She'd planned to be attending the same balls as before, though this time nobody would let her take refuge behind curtains. She had not planned to be on a ship that glided through the Thames, and that would soon glide over the English Channel.

No one, not even Flora, had asked Charlotte so many questions about herself. She'd told him that her heart hurt during stress, and he seemed determined to alleviate stress—even the kind that occurred to her and was not obvious to everyone else. Through all if his questions, he'd seemed kind. His lips might have twitched, but he seemed to be smiling *with* her. She seemed to know he would never share what she said with anyone else.

More passengers gathered on the deck, observing the sailors. The ship swept through the Thames and moved past dockyards.

A well-dressed man and woman eyed them. The woman had the sort of caramel colored hair that was just unique enough to merit some attention. Her dress was stylish, and her figure was in all the fashionable proportions.

"Duke of Vernon?" The well-dressed man raised his eyebrows in evident surprise. Not a loose hair was visible, and they must have been perfectly plucked. He waved.

"I'll introduce you," Callum said to Charlotte and offered her his arm.

Charlotte rested her hand in the crook of his elbow. It felt good, even if the short walk did not merit physical assistance. The floorboards were clean, and unlike on land, there was not even a hint of mud on which her feet might slide.

"My dear, Charlotte," Callum said, "please let me introduce you to Lord Braunschweig. Lord Braunschweig, this is Miss Charlotte Butterworth."

"I am most delighted to meet you," Lord Braunschweig said, in a silky baritone that Charlotte did not trust at all, despite the consistency with which the man smiled.

"Though she will soon be the Duchess of Vernon," Callum said, and the man's eyes seemed to snap in surprise.

"You are eloping."

"Correct," Callum answered."

"How...romantic," Lord Braunschweig said, and Charlotte felt that even in her wedding finery she didn't quite meet the expectations of the *ton.* Finally, the man gestured to his female companion. "Please let me present my sister."

"I am delighted to meet you both." The woman practically purred. She lifted an elegant hand to her throat and retained a cool and composed smile that reminded Charlotte every bit of Lady Isla.

Charlotte tried to act nonchalant, and she forced a smile.

The steward reappeared. "Your rooms are prepared, Your Grace. I have taken the liberty of informing the captain that you are on the ship. You will take your meals with him."

"Thank you," Callum said.

The steward led them below the deck as the ship left the most crowded part of the Thames. The steward introduced them to the captain. Despite their late and unexpected arrival, everyone seemed happy for them to be on board. They would be on the ship for a few days, and sailors generally sailed for weeks. And yet a few days from land seemed far away. She could hardly swim back to London, should the boat capsize. One had to completely trust the actions of the captain.

Chapter Fifteen

THEY WOULD ARRIVE IN Guernsey today.

Excitement thrummed through Charlotte, but she focused on the accounts that Callum had brought with him from Hades' Lair. Numbers were comforting, but these numbers were also fascinating. Callum's former guardian had been most devious.

Footsteps padded outside her cabin, and a knock sounded.

She opened the door, and Callum stood before her. "We're nearing Saint Peter Port. Would you like to see?"

"Oh, indeed." She closed the door and followed him through the narrow corridor, nearly stumbling as the waves continued to rock the ship.

Callum turned around and steadied her, and his arms felt secure and unwavering.

The door was at the top of a long wooden staircase, and Charlotte knew it would probably be more pleasant to wait for the boat to dock. Still, she pushed the door open without any hesitation.

Cold air brushed against her, and for a moment, she trembled. The wind seemed determined to lift up her hem, and she was thankful for the heavy fabric of the traveling gown Flora had packed and its relative narrowness.

"Don't blow away, lass," he murmured, his voice husky, and he took her hand.

Normally the man didn't use Scottish words, even though traces of his burr were present every time he spoke.

A shiver of excitement rushed through Charlotte.

The man's handsomeness was the sort that extended through him. He was good and wanted the best for everyone. She needed to remind herself of the latter point. It was almost possible to imagine that they were a couple eloping because they were madly in love, and not simply because it was convenient to both of them. The reasons for their marriage could hardly be termed romantic, no matter Callum's pleasant demeanor and the appealing composition of his facial features.

Salty spray spilled onto the deck and dappled her dress and face, and she inhaled the scent. Her locks whipped across her face, the pins having long since lost their usefulness after the days-long battle with the elements.

A green island spread out before them. The channel was gray, but it didn't diminish the wonder of the steep cliffs that sloped around the sea, forming delightful bays and coves.

"That's Guernsey." Callum pointed in the distance.

At first, Charlotte didn't see anything. The waves sufficed in beauty. Foamy crests rose toward the sky, as if competing with one another in a never-ending tournament.

They needn't. The water alone was beautiful. The pale blue managed to contain shades of green. Were the color discovered in a jewel, it would triumph over any other.

There before them, growing increasingly taller, was an island. White cliffs rose in the distance, but unlike the waves, these did not simply collapse into the ocean. If the waves desired to rival anything, no target could be more magnificent than this land. The ship veered toward it, and pastel-colored homes perched about a harbor. The sailors' activities shifted and grew more vigorous.

Callum squeezed her hand. "We're almost there."

Salty water continued to spray her face, but she didn't step away.

Tiny fishing boats dipped over the sea, and people sat in them. The world was filled with more than the ocean and the sky, even though both of those seemed incredible.

"We'll be married soon," Callum said.

Those words might be meant to be reassuring, but her heartbeat quickened all the same.

Marriage had seemed a good idea. It had seemed novel, exciting, a stage of life which she had so nearly missed. But now it was truly happening.

She wanted to stay on this ship forever, admiring the azure color of the ocean and conscious of Callum beside her. The sky was a crisp blue, devoid of any of the clouds that seemed to delight in flittering about England's skies, striking unease in anyone beneath them who might ponder to themselves, whether that shade of gray, that precise form of fluffiness, was likely to lead to rain, and if so, at what time they might expect it on even the nicest, sunniest days in Norfolk.

Finally, the ship halted.

Geese strutted over the shore, directing their beaks to the ground and vigilantly pecking whichever edible delight they happened upon. The water was calm, and the boats left triangular ripples in the water. Sailboats glided through the water with the elegance of swans, spurred by the steadiness of the wind's pace. Fishing nets hung from some boats, appearing like lace.

"I didn't think this could be Britain," Charlotte murmured.

Callum gave her a pleased smile, the sort unaccompanied by worried lines about his eyes.

"Follow me," Callum said, disembarking from the ship. Charlotte was conscious of the captain and Lord Braunschweig and his sister following them.

"I thought you'd never been here before," Charlotte said.

"I haven't," Callum said, "but there's a church there."

"Oh."

This was it.

"Stop!" A voice barreled after them. "You can't get married."

They were the same words Callum's brother had uttered, and for a wild moment she considered the possibility his brother might have followed them.

But this man's accent was decidedly not Scottish.

Georgiana tensed and she turned round slowly.

It was the captain.

The man wrinkled his brow, and his nostrils flared.

"You can't get married," the captain repeated, and Callum squeezed Charlotte's hand.

"You can't prevent us from marrying," Callum.

"I wouldn't dream of preventing your match," the captain said solemnly. "It's so lovely to see such a nice couple."

Charlotte blinked. It wouldn't have occurred to her that bushy-bearded sea captains used words like lovely.

"A pretty girl like that won't want to go straight to the chapel, no matter how besotted you are. You need a celebration."

"Oh, yes," Lord Braunschweig's sister said, clapping her hands together. "A wedding is the happiest day of your life. It should be perfect. It must be perfect."

"And perfect starts with?"

"Flowers," Lord Braunschweig's sister said. "I'll get some guests and speak with the preacher."

Charlotte felt uncharitable that she'd been suspicious of her. She might still be uneasy around Lord Braunschweig, but perhaps a woman's propensity to wear nice attire did not mean they had a propensity to not be nice.

THE WEDDING WAS PERFECT.

It wasn't Mayfair, and no Grecian columns adorned the single-story church that squatted in the center of the town, as if weighted down by its steeple. The stained-glass windows were of the small variety, and their existence dimmed the small amount of light that streamed through the panes.

And yet, the stone floor reminded her of her father's chapel. The place was all medieval charm. Charlotte's heart swelled. If only this weren't the end. If only she weren't dying. If only...

"Ready?" Callum whispered.

"Yes," Charlotte said.

Callum gestured, and music started playing. Wild flowers adorned the chapel.

Charlotte blinked. "It's beautiful."

The music played, and soon the vicar spoke.

Chapter Sixteen

CALLUM WISHED HE COULD take Charlotte to the finest palace. They'd celebrated their wedding, but it was now evening. He supposed the inn's room at least had the advantage of not rocking, even if the curtains were a drab brown that would never be found at even the most modest manors.

The bed lay in the center of the room. Though no silk sheets peeked from it, and no embroidered fabrics draped over it, his pulse still quickened. A strange image of throwing Charlotte onto the bed overcame him.

He avoided her gaze, as if she could read his emotions.

They hadn't made a love match, and even if they had, the doctor had expressly instructed that Charlotte could experience no excitement.

The light from the lantern flickered over her skin, giving it a delightful golden hue. His eyes danced about the room, landing everywhere except her.

"I'll—er—sleep in the next room of course," Callum said. "I hope it will be suitable for you."

"Naturally," Charlotte said.

"Please let me know if you require anything," Callum said. "At any time. Please do not hesitate at all."

"I wouldn't expect you to stay in your room," Charlotte said softly.

"What do you mean?"

She swept her long lashes downward. "Only that you're a man, and you appear to be one in possession of virility."

"I don't understand."

"Men's cravings," she said. "I do know about them. I might be untouched, but I'm not naïve."

Untouched.

There should be a law against women like her saying such a word. The only thought running through his head now was touching her. He desired to touch her...everywhere.

She was beautiful.

Somehow, she had no idea, probably because men like him had dismissed her, sensing there was something about the cut of her dress, the choice of her fabric, and the way she was never seen in the same circles as the most distinguished debutantes, that made her unworthy.

"I don't expect you to uphold your marriage vows," she said.

THE MAN MANAGED TO evoke such shock and innocence that Charlotte blushed.

"The thought isn't so ridiculous," she said.

"You're expecting me to spend the night with someone I just met instead of my own wife?"

She swallowed hard. "We don't have that kind of marriage." She raised her chin. "I-I'm open minded about such things. I understand men's needs."

"Whom exactly do you think I would like to see? Some woman on the dockyard?"

She hesitated. "Perhaps the baron's sister. She seems quite sophisticated."

"Nonsense. Why would my needs include her?"

Charlotte knew the answer to this question. She raised her chin. "The baron's sister is a beautiful woman."

"Is she?" Callum seemed amused.

Charlotte frowned. He wasn't taking this seriously.

"Yes, her features are quite symmetrical. Her hair is golden."

"So is yours," Callum said.

"But mine is flaxen. It can't be described as golden."

"It's rarer," Callum said. "Far more special."

Charlotte flushed. Why was the man looking at her like that? He shouldn't look at her like that. It made her yearn for other things. Things that were impossible.

"And she's tall," Charlotte said, conscious that for some reason her voice was squeaking. "Statuesque."

"I don't want a statue." Callum narrowed the distance between them.

"I mean of course not," Charlotte said, laughing, though the sound seemed awkward. "That would be ridiculous. What would you do with a statue?"

"What indeed?" Callum said, and the man's eyes glimmered for a reason she couldn't quite define. Most likely, it involved something sultry.

"I only meant her height is similar to you. You might find it convenient."

"Convenient?" he sputtered.

"Mathematically. A similar height would mean a smaller distance for kissing. Far more convenient. I'm surprised the thought has never occurred to you before."

"I remember us kissing," he said.

Fire blazed through her. The room was getting far too warm, despite the steady ocean breeze, and despite the fact that the sun had gone down long before.

She remembered too.

She remembered everything about those few seconds. She remembered the exact sweep of his lips and the exact manner in which his tongue had briefly touched hers. She remembered his scent, and she remembered the brush of his cheek against hers. She even remembered how his arm had briefly grazed hers.

"Differences in heights are no barrier," Callum murmured.

"No?" she breathed.

"No." Callum was only inches from her, and in one sudden, glorious movement, he pulled her into his arms, as effortlessly as if he were holding a book.

Her heart soared, conscious of the touch of his arm against her back and under her legs. She might be fully clothed, but the action was utterly intimate. His shirt stretched in interesting manners, some of the linen fabric caught by her dress, and she was aware of his muscles. The thin linen was no true barrier.

He was taller than she was. Most people were taller than she was, but her world was now consumed with the view of the broad shoulders and his face, gazing at her. If she looked at him she would consumed with contemplating the man's chiseled features, his straight nose and chin, and his high cheekbones that light seemed to desire to dance over, as if each sunbeam knew that there could be no nicer spot than him. He raked a hand through his curly blond locks. He managed to seem exasperated, a quality she was sure he should not possess.

"The thing is," he said, his voice husky. "I'm not going to visit the baron's sister."

"But her qualities are remarkable."

"Her qualities are irrelevant. I have what matters in my arms."

She jerked her head toward him, and he set her down.

HE'D SAID TOO MUCH.

The fact was obvious.

Her eyes were widening at an alarming rate.

His words had been spontaneous, not thought out, though he had the uncomfortable sensation that did not render them any less true.

He swallowed hard.

She couldn't be what mattered to him most. She hadn't agreed to a love match.

"What are you thinking?" she asked.

The images that raced through his mind were not images one shared with a maiden. And yet, the curve of her collarbone seemed utterly enticing, and he was filled with an urge to follow the curve to her bodice. What would she appear like? Freed from the ridiculous clothes her mother had put her in? Freed from the more tailored dress she'd worn to their wedding that never was?

What would be the shape of her peaks? Would they be rosy? Or a more tawny shade? He longed to glide his hand over them and feel them pebble beneath him.

Her hair dangled over his hand. The tresses were silky. Charlotte's hair was always up, tied into a sensible updo which no doubt made for easier explorations of nature, but now it was loose and utterly enticing.

He couldn't let her think she was in any way less than any other member of the *ton*. Her interests were so varied, so intense. He didn't need to be with someone who knew the answers to every single line, who knew the steps to every dance, or who knew how to address everyone appropriately.

He'd been bored by the woman of the *ton*. They'd been beautiful, shimmering in their Parisian gowns, even at the height of war when the only people going to France should have been spies, intent on dismantling the brutal regime, rather than people intent on discovering the latest trends in fashion.

Charlotte was different.

He gazed at her again, and her lashes fluttered downward.

He couldn't allow her to think she was anything less than wonderful. He stroked her hair, and he still held her in his arms.

"You are beautiful," he said.

"And you are kind," she said.

"That's more than you would have said about me when we first met."

"You've not made any carriage invasions since then," she said, and humor glimmered in her pale blue eyes.

Nervousness, certainly, was not a trait Callum was familiar with. Nervousness was something confined to other men with less pleasing features, whose skin was less exquisite, whose height could never be termed lofty, and whose shoulders would always be termed narrow, no matter how much they might throw themselves into playing squash or perch on a galloping horse.

But gazing down at Charlotte, nervousness thundered through Callum all the same.

He kissed her.

His lips brushed against hers, and life was magnificent.

I mustn't.

The woman was dying. Sudden excitement could cause her deadly harm.

He wanted her to take pleasure in life, not endanger her.

"I—er—should leave," he said hastily. "I'll be in the next room."

He hastened through the adjoining door. His heart thumped madly, as if intent on admonishing him for leaving her.

Chapter Seventeen

THE NEXT DAY SUNBEAMS splattered through the thin curtains of the room, and a strip of cerulean blue ocean was visible through Charlotte's window. Unfortunately, neither image managed to banish the memory of her husband sprinting from her bedroom like a petty thief the night before, and she made her way warily down the steps.

The innkeeper ushered her to the breakfast room. Charlotte had stopped in posting inns with her family on their way to Norfolk, but those had been filled with groggy-eyed travelers attempting to barrel sufficient food into their mouths with efficiency. This place exuded calm, and the innkeeper led her to a table.

"The spread looks delicious," she said.

"I am very glad, Your Grace."

Your Grace.

It was the first time someone had referred to her as such, and she attempted to act calmly, as if those were words she'd always heard, as if those were words that she'd always assumed would be her destiny. She spread dark apple butter on a roll, proud that her knife did not wobble.

"The duke should be out shortly," the innkeeper continued, and Charlotte despised the flurry of butterflies that seemed to flutter against her spine.

If she'd had any doubts on the duke's dashingness, their kiss would have dismissed them. They'd kissed, and unlike last time, he had not done so on the bidding of someone else. For a blissful moment, everything had been utterly wonderful.

It was still utterly wonderful, she reminded herself.

"Ah, Your Grace."

"Charlotte." Callum's deep voice rumbled, and she turned around. "How did you sleep?"

"Rather well," she said. "And you?"

Their conversation felt stilted, but the images that flashed through her mind were anything but ordinary. What would have happened had Callum stayed?

It would be most convenient if the man were not nearly so handsome. She shouldn't be pondering the manner in which his shirt tightened over his chest. Even though he'd evidently found a pair of buckskins, and no proprietress in her right mind would have permitted him entry to Almack's with his casual attire—even if he were titled—he emanated charm. His tailcoat didn't quite fit him, but that only gave him a boyish appeal. She grabbed another roll and lathered black butter onto it. It wouldn't do to contemplate the way his muscles had felt beneath his shirt and tailcoat last night, and how their height difference hadn't truly mattered after all when he'd held her in his arms.

"I'm going to take you exploring the island today," he announced.

"Oh?"

"Have you been fishing?"

"Naturally not. Besides, that's not a ladylike venture."

He leaned closer to her. "I know it's not. That's why I thought you might like it."

"I think there might be an insult in that."

"There's not. Only a compliment." He winked, and the action seemed to cause those butterflies to invade her chest again, as if the man managed to conjure them with his mere gaze. "Now hurry up. Let's go."

She made herself ready quickly, and soon they strode through Saint Peter Port.

"Are you quite fond of fishing?" she asked.

"Not excessively fond," he said. "I haven't fished in a while. But I used to. Quite frequently."

"In the Highlands."

"No better fishing in the world," he declared.

"Then why haven't you been back in years?"

He turned to her, and the glimmer in his eyes disappeared. "How did you know I haven't been back in years?"

"I may have overheard Lord Braunschweig speaking about it. He had an invitation to go to Scotland, but he was pondering not attending."

"And he stated my lack of recent visits as a reason for him not to visit?"

"Precisely," she said, but her voice wobbled.

The pleasant expression on Callum's face vanished, and he raked his hand through his hair. "My reasons for not liking Scotland have nothing to do with anyone else. They are personal."

She stiffened. "You don't have to explain."

"Thank you," Callum said quietly.

They passed pastel-colored stone homes. Seagulls darted above them, but the world seemed somewhat less idyllic than before. Charlotte lengthened her steps, and soon they left the small town and strode into open fields, dotted with distant farmhouses. Clouds fluttered over the sky.

"The secret to fishing is good fishing tackle," Callum declared.

"I'd rather assumed it was finding a good location," Charlotte said.

"That too," Callum said. "You already show talent."

Charlotte giggled. "Are we going to get poles?"

"I thought we would just throw spears into the water."

Charlotte must have looked surprised, for Callum grinned. "Guernsey's style of fishing is not that different from the type favored in Britain."

"The other sort will still be a novel experience for me."

Callum led them to a small cottage and emerged with fishing supplies. His hair was tousled, and his buckskins already muddy from their walk. He looked nothing like the polished, aloof aristocrat she'd seen at Sir Seymour's ball.

"You love nature," she observed.

"I suppose I do."

"Why didn't you join the navy?" Charlotte murmured.

"I was too worried they might send me to Virginia and battle in an unnecessary war with the former colonies."

"Oh."

"Blood shouldn't be spilled casually. France was where the real battle was. I wasn't going to punish some fresh-faced youths whose ancestors had had the temerity to fight for a fraction of the freedom I have."

"That's very noble."

"I have my moments." Callum's eyes glimmered, and Charlotte turned away and shaded her face. No need for him to know that his gaze exceeded sunrays in strength.

Callum led her over an increasingly rocky path, toward the sound of a river. "Tell me if it becomes strenuous."

"I'm fine," Charlotte said.

Charlotte might be nervous around other people, but rivers were rather less intimidating.

"I thought you might prefer this to spending the rest of the day with Lord Braunschweig and his sister," Callum said.

"You supposed correctly."

"Excellent." They rounded a bend, and a small stream lay before them. The water moved quickly, as if eager to reach the channel.

Charlotte stared at the clear water. "It's beautiful."

"Good," Callum said. "Then let's start here."

Charlotte took a seat on a rock, and Callum settled casually beside her, before proceeding to tell her about the complexities of fishing tackle. Happiness thrummed through her.

THE DAYS WERE LONG and filled with sunshine. Charlotte and Callum explored the island. In the evenings, they sometimes dined with Lord Braunschweig and his sister, but mostly they were together. Callum should miss London. He'd been able to indulge in all the city had to offer, but he realized it was the countryside which he craved.

Charlotte and he had taken a boat to explore the other side the island. They pulled the boat onto the shore and then strode through the idyllic landscape. Charlotte exclaimed over the variety of flowers.

"I must confess to having grown quite fond of hills," Charlotte said.

"You don't miss Norfolk?"

"I miss my family."

Callum swallowed hard, and her eyes softened.

"I'm sorry," she said gently. "You must miss your family too."

"They've been gone a long time," Callum said.

"That doesn't make it better."

No.

It didn't.

"How did they die?" she asked.

"It's my fault they're gone," he confessed.

He stiffened.

He hadn't meant to tell her that. He'd never told anyone that.

"What on earth do you mean?" she asked.

"It's nothing." He glanced at the landscape. "This almost reminds me of Scotland."

"Callum," she said sternly. "How could it possibly be your fault that they died? I hardly imagine you spent your youth murdering relatives."

"Then perhaps you should broaden your imagination," he said glumly.

Her eyes widened, and he sighed. "I'll tell you. I-I hope you won't think worse of me, but I understand if you will."

"Heavens. What is troubling you?"

"I acted poorly as a child," he said. "I was...naughty."

Her eyebrows rose. "Most children are naughty."

"I doubt you were."

She flushed. "I enjoyed the indoors."

"Anyway. I was naughty. I didn't listen to my parents. I played with everyone, even the local children. Even when I was expressly told not to," his voice wobbled. "I'd disobeyed them before. But this time—" His lips twisted, and his voice had become hoarse.

Charlotte rested her palm against his shoulder, the same action that she might have done with her sister, and he eased into the sensation, as if to draw strength from their sudden intimacy.

"The next door children were sick. My parents didn't want me to get sick. They were right," he said shortly, jerking his head away from her.

She squeezed his arm gently. "But you're fine now."

He swung around. "But they're not. They're dead. Don't you see? It was my fault. If I hadn't played with them, I wouldn't have gotten sick, and then my parents wouldn't have died."

His voice sounded hollow, and she longed to pull him toward her. Instead, she squeezed his hand.

"You didn't know," she said.

"I was warned," he said bitterly.

"If you had been told your parents would die if you disobeyed them, I'm certain you wouldn't have."

His shoulders seemed to relax. "You're right."

"Of course I am."

He tilted his head toward her. "Thank you. No one else knows."

"Not your brother?"

He shook his head vehemently. "I wouldn't want my brother to know."

"He would understand," she said.

"The one person who knew was not understanding."

"You said no one else knew."

He looked away. "He's dead now. Lord McIntyre. My guardian."

She frowned. "And he was unkind."

He gave a harsh laugh. "He used it. He promised to keep my secret, while threatening to tell Hamish.

"I'm so very sorry."

He stared at her, fighting the urge to kiss her. She hadn't run away. She didn't appear horrified. She just seemed utterly lovely.

Perhaps she was correct.

Chapter Eighteen

TWO WEEKS PASSED. THEY'D only gone to Guernsey because of Callum's brother's behavior, and Guernsey's status as a suitable elopement destination, but he was pleased that they had come here.

"Are you happy?" he asked as they strolled through Saint Peter Port.

She gave a wobbly smile, and Callum cursed himself. Of course, she couldn't be simply happy. Not when her physician had given her a death sentence. No amount of vibrant, blooming flowers, no amount of sunshine spattered shorelines, no amount of crisp blue water, could change that.

"I am happy," she said. "More than I thought possible."

His shoulders relaxed, and he beamed. "Splendid. We can explore the other islands. Jersey is supposed to be quite spectacular."

She smiled, but something about it made him gaze at her sharply.

"You want to return?"

She nodded. "This has been so marvelous, but my parents..."

His heart clenched again. "I could send for them."

"I don't want to worry them."

"They must know sometime."

"I-I know."

Charlotte's illness hung between them.

Callum led Charlotte to the harbor. A ship towered over the cheerfully painted fishing boats docked at Saint Peter Port and emanated sophistication. Sailors in striped shirts moved decisively over the deck, repeating steps they had made their whole lives.

"If you would like, we can take this ship tomorrow morning. Lord Braunschweig and his sister are planning to travel back to London on it. It's smaller than the one we came here on and it only goes to Portsmouth. But we could take the ship and then take a carriage from Portsmouth to London, stopping to visit my manor house in Hampshire. We can wait for the larger ship of course, but that departs in five days, so we would reach London at the same time. I thought you might enjoy seeing more things."

"That sounds splendid."

Charlotte tilted her head, and her blond locks billowed in the breeze. Her smile had seemed to grow more serious. "Are you certain?"

"Yes. But we are going to take you to every specialist the city has."

"Doctor Hutton is the best."

He stopped. She was right. Everyone knew the doctor's reputation.

It was excellent.

"Then I will take your whole family to Bath and drag you to all the best doctors there. And then to Tunbridge. And then to Harrogate."

Charlotte's eyes widened, and he kneeled beside her.

Blast it.

He was going to tell her. These two weeks had been amazing. He wanted to tell her that she'd become everything to him.

That he adored her. That he *loved* her.

The words hung on the tips of his lips to be released.

But still...

He hesitated.

Would her lips quiver and would she admit similar feelings? Or would she grow more pale, unsure how to tell him that his feelings were not reciprocated?

He didn't want her to feel forced. They'd entered the marriage without love, with a careful contract, and he didn't desire to change the terms on her, and make her live as if it were a love match for her.

After all, she'd just declared a desire to return to England.

She'd been so cool and collected when she'd outlined the terms to him.

So instead, he turned toward the ship. "I'll purchase us tickets."

She nodded, and he hurried up the gangway, unsure what sorts of secrets he might reveal, were he to remain in her presence.

He craved her.

He yearned for her.

Images of her flashed through his head constantly, whether she was before him or not, and he smiled when he remembered their conversations. There were so many things he wanted to show her, but when he was with her, he was not nearly as articulate as he associated himself with. His tongue seemed to thicken, and his words did not leave his mouth in elegant flourishes.

He'd told her his deepest secret, and she hadn't been shocked. She hadn't abhorred him, and she hadn't even looked at him differently. She'd only squeezed his hand and murmured sweet things to him.

CHARLOTTE AND HE WERE sailing toward London, but the ship seemed to be making its very best attempt at ensuring disaster. The waves seemed to have mistaken the ship for a cricket ball, and each wave seemed to be under the assumption it was a cricket bat and seemed determined to each fling the ship farther than the other.

It was all Callum's fault. If only he hadn't suggested to take Charlotte to the Channel Islands. A woman like her should be safe, on the ground, where no water could flood her surroundings, and no wooden walls might break apart about her, hurling splinters at her with the nonchalance of a rain shower.

He shouldn't have allowed his brother to thwart Charlotte's and his carefully planned wedding day, and he certainly shouldn't have suggested they elope on an island.

The furniture might be fastened to the walls, but the pillow had developed a habit of flying to odd corners of the room, and the only reason the blanket hadn't joined was because Callum and Charlotte were clutching onto it.

Charlotte.

He was very aware of her presence.

His thoughts should have been focused on visions of impending death.

That would have been logical, despite his reassurances to Charlotte.

He'd been in storms before, but never ones of quite such intensity. Never ones that pitched the ship in every direction. If he had a less strong stomach, he might have been experiencing physical agony, but the only distraction in this cabin was Charlotte.

Her body was thin and petite and perfect.

His body seemed to be delighting in her presence, despite the fact death seemed to be peering infuriatingly close. She'd pressed her small hands against his chest, as if his ribs alone would give her comfort.

Well, she was not wrong to do that.

He would do damn everything he could to protect her.

If the ship sank into the water, he would haul her in his arms and carry her through the water-filled corridors so they might escape into the ocean. This vessel was not going to become their coffin. If the ship split, if lightning struck the great mast, he would swim with her to safety. No waves, no matter their strength, could lessen his resolve to protect her.

She's everything.

The lantern crashed, and he blinked into inky darkness. Broken glass rattled on the floor, and he clutched her closer to him.

Her breasts pressed against his side. They were soft and alluring, and his body ached with an urge to run his fingers over them, to clasp them, to kiss them.

How had he possibly dismissed her?

He moved his hand gently over her body, as if to ascertain that she was really there beside him.

EVERYTHING WAS DARK, and everything should have been dreadful.

The ship, for all its modern wonders of constructions, was struggling. The thunderstorm roared above them, and she clasped Callum more tightly.

Callum.

She shouldn't be looking for him for comfort.

She shouldn't be so predictable.

Perhaps he was her husband, but they both knew he'd not taken on the position out of a desire to hold her through the night.

She removed her hands from his chest and inched toward the end of the bed.

The task was not difficult.

The bed's width was of the narrow variety; it was not meant for two people. She should never have succumbed to her fear to begin with, should never have joined him here at all.

Thunder sounded again. Its low baritone rumbled over her. Sailors shouted above them, and she imagined lightning rushing down from the sky, the silver streaks illuminating for a terrifying second the crashing of the waves against the ship. Had the lighting struck the ship? She froze.

All the money of the ship magnate who'd built this ship, all the centuries of knowledge on ship building, all the decades of skill of the sailors—if nature decided to have a ferocious storm, none of those things could prevent the destruction of the ship and all of their deaths.

How arbitrary life could be. How very odd the duke had happened to spot her cart, had happened to require a bride, and they'd married and ended up here together. When they'd sailed to Guernsey, the crossing had been calm and smooth, but now the whole world had shifted.

No stars would be visible now. The sky would be opaque, and no one would be wondering at the world's beauty, only at its power.

"Charlotte?" Rustling sounded. "You can be closer. If you want."

Charlotte was silent, and she fought the temptation to roll back into his arms and grasped onto the end of the bed.

She couldn't allow herself to be seen as so vulnerable. Would he be laughing to himself at the manner in which she would clutch him toward herself? Would he be uncomfortable, bracing himself through the experience as he might during a particularly unpleasant meeting at his club?

"You can't be comfortable," he said again.

The ship continued to pitch, as if to push her toward him, and she tightened her hands on the bed, as the ship rolled through the waves, fighting gravity's determination to topple her toward the floor.

"I see," Callum said, his voice more quiet. "*I* can go on the floor."

"There's glass on the floor," she said quickly. The man shouldn't hurt himself.

The thunder roared again, more ferocious than any lion, and the world shook. She tightened her grip again, but this time even she could not stay on the bed.

She pitched over the ledge, and despite her instincts to retain some semblance of dignity, she squealed.

In the next moment, strong arms were around her, pulling her toward him. She wrapped her arms around him instinctively, noting the breadth of his chest and inhaling his masculine scent.

She forced her eyes shut, but the room was already dark, and no change occurred. Nothing could banish the man's comforting clasp on her or his appealing scent.

"I'm not going to let anything happen to you," he said soothingly.

"We're going to die," she said.

"Nonsense," he said, and he managed to sound so utterly confident she smiled.

"That is not the plan for tonight," he said.

"Then what is?" Her voice wobbled, and she felt blood rush to her cheeks.

At least the room was dark.

At least he couldn't see her.

But the blanket rustled again, and he came closer to her.

"This is," he said, in his tenor voice.

In the next moment, she was being kissed.

Callum had kissed her before, of course.

Those kisses had been strong and forceful, highlighting a passion she wasn't supposed to feel, and one which she knew he certainly did not feel. Those kisses normally were the province of milkmaids and shepherds, people who didn't need to abide by society's rules.

This kiss was tender, despite the hammer of waves against the ship. The world might be turning this way and that, threatening to sink into an abyss of salty water, inhabited by vicious, unseeing sea creatures and the algae upon which they typically satisfied themselves, but right now, Callum was beside her and life felt not nearly as threatening.

Heavens, she craved him.

The man's salty scent tantalized her nostrils, and she adored the rough feel of his cheeks as they brushed against hers. Shaving was not advisable during turbulent seas, and she felt a thrill to witness him in a state not seen by others in the *ton*.

This was Callum, and right now, he was hers.

At least, he seemed to be giving every indication of desiring to be hers.

His lips brushed against hers. The touch was so gentle it ushered an undulation of yearning through her.

His mouth moved everywhere. He claimed her cheeks, her throat, even her earlobes.

Everything sent tremors rushing through her. He was beside her, on top of her, and life was absolutely heavenly.

"How do you feel?" he asked.

"I'm fine," she said.

And she was. Her heart didn't hurt, and her breath didn't come out in strange bursts.

"I should stop," he said, but she didn't miss the hint of longing, the hint of regret emitted through his voice.

So she swept him into her arms. This time she kissed him. This time her lips sought his. She repeated the movements his lips had made, but this time there was more, as if her action had caused him to unrestrain himself, like a horse freed from an unwelcome harness and eager to gallop about a field.

Well.

She should feel more hesitant. The doctor had been clear that she was to have no excitement. And yet the only thing that seemed to be possible to cause her to distress was to not be with him, to not feel him beside him, to not clutch him, to not have his lips claim hers, his hands—

The man's hands were moving in a most intriguing fashion about her.

"You're so beautiful," he murmured.

"The lantern is out."

He chuckled. "I haven't forgotten your appearance. Besides, I can feel you." He brushed his fingers over her body, as if finding pleasure in her mere shape.

The sky thundered again, but this time it seemed fainter. She wasn't certain whether it was because they were moving from the storm, or if Callum had such power over her.

She smiled.

Of course, he had such power.

I love him.

Chapter Nineteen

NERVOUSNESS, CERTAINLY, was not a trait Callum was familiar with. Nervousness was something confined to other men with less pleasing features, whose skin was less exquisite, whose height could never be termed lofty, and whose shoulders would always be termed narrow, no matter how much they might throw themselves into playing squash or perch on a galloping horse.

But nervousness thundered through Callum all the same.

I shouldn't touch her.

Excitement could be fatal. The doctor's apprentice had been specific. How could he harm her? *I love her.*

The words rose up unbidden in his mind, and he kept them unspoken.

Not touching her was impossible. Not when she moaned sweetly, not when her arms clung onto him, and not when she whispered his first name on her tongue.

He wanted her. He desired her. He yearned for her.

He found her mouth again with his, and he allowed himself to succumb to their tongues' rhythm.

"Do you think...?" He halted. He shouldn't suggest it. He shouldn't suggest actually bedding her.

It didn't matter that she was his wife, and consummating a marriage was normally a venture taken on in the first night. It didn't matter even that he

"What is it?" she asked. Her voice sounded almost...hopeful.

"I don't want to hurt you," he said.

She laughed softly. "I rather think the storm is more likely to hurt me."

"I won't let that happen," he said defiantly, and his hands tightened into fists, as if he might tackle the storm with the enthusiasm of a boxer.

"I know," she said reassuringly.

And then, sweet heavens, she kissed him again.

He'd already memorized the curves of her slender body, but now his hands explored everywhere.

If he were doing this properly, he would have wanted candlelight everywhere and to be with her on a luxurious bed. The narrow bed of the ship was imperfect, especially given its recent propensity to tip. He held onto her. He wasn't going to allow her to fall.

He kept his mouth on her, exploring her succulent lips and the soft curve of her cheeks and neck. He wanted to claim every inch of her skin. He grasped her tightly to him, and continued to kiss her while he moved his other hand to explore her hips, her thighs, her bottom.

He pulled himself from her lips, instantly missing their delicious taste. "I want to be inside you."

He paused, not sure if she understood. He'd never been with someone untouched before.

But Charlotte only squeezed him more tightly. "Yes. Oh, yes."

His hardness strained against his falls, begging to be freed. The feel of Charlotte in his arms had turned him to stone long ago. He undid the buttons quickly, and he lifted her skirts. He pulled her drawers down, and more pleasure rushed through his body as his fingers touched the delicate shape of her legs.

Heavens, she was tiny. So delicate. So utterly perfect.

"I love you," she said, wrapping her arms about his neck. "I think it's appropriate that you know."

"Sweetheart," he murmured. "I love you too."

She'd uttered the words he'd felt.

He moved his hands over her again, concentrating on the delightful curve of her breasts.

"My bosom is small," she said.

"Your bosom is perfect," he said huskily, and she sighed. .

He glided his hand over her chest. His hands brushed over her peaks, and her body trembled.

"Keep on doing that," she said.

"It's my absolute pleasure," he said.

Heaven, it seemed, was right here on this ship, with Charlotte. Her hands tentatively explored his body, and then, he moved his fingers to her entrance, delving into warmth and wonderfulness.

"Oooh," she murmured.

"Is that nice?"

"Exceedingly so," she declared.

Heavens.

She couldn't say those things to him. His length seemed to harden even more, and he removed his fingers. This time, when he entered her, it would be with his most intimate part.

"Tell me if it hurts," he warned.

"Very well."

He pressed into her, and everything was perfect. Pleasure soared through his mind, and he rocked inside her. He dipped his face toward hers, and continued to kiss her.

The waves sloshed against the hull, and the thunder raged above them. It didn't matter.

All that mattered was Charlotte.

Joy surged through him, and he pulled out rapidly and spilled his seed over her. He then moved his fingers over her entrance, until she trembled and moaned.

"Sweetheart," he said again, clutching her closely to him.

SCREAMING JOLTED CHARLOTTE from her reverie.

There had been screaming before, but not like this.

Grown men in her experience did not scream. In the next moment a crash sounded, as if dozens of brooms were snapping apart.

Heavens.

The room tilted, and Callum grasped hold of her.

"Everyone out!" a sailor shouted. "Go! Go! Go!"

Oh, no.

Callum grabbed Charlotte and pulled her toward the door, despite the darkness, despite the horrible sounds of the storm and the shouting sailors. Water sloshed in from above, even though no water should be here.

This was not the nice upright ship she'd encountered in the port, and it certainly wasn't the majestic quick sailing one, with all its sails carefully sewn, billowing proudly in the wind.

This ship was a disaster.

This was a catastrophe.

The world tilted more.

Is this death?

Is this the last thing I'll remember?

Somewhere she could hear Callum saying her name, and then he swore and swept her into his arms. She wrapped her arms around his neck.

The ship rocked violently, forcing them against the walls. Finally, Callum put her in front of the narrow staircase.

"Climb up, sweetheart," he said gently.

"Quickly!" Lord Braunschweig's voice bellowed behind her. "The ship is sinking! *Mein Gott*!"

"You have your sister?" Callum called out.

"I'm behind you," Miss Braunschweig said.

Charlotte's heart beat wildly, and she pulled herself up the stairs.

The wind slammed against her, accompanied by thousands of raindrops that seemed to have shifted into a horizontal direction. Her eyes stung, and she wasn't sure if it was because of the rain or her own tears.

The mast was missing. That had been the crash. It had likely rolled off the ship.

The deck groaned beneath her, and a prickle of additional fear ran through her body.

Perhaps she was alive, perhaps she was not really sick, but could she die now anyway? And this time not simply months before her time, but decades?

She glanced at Callum. The man had a grim look to his face "The deck is going to collapse," he said.

Oh.

Fear gripped her.

"In here! In here!" The captain pointed to a wooden boat.

Callum swept her into his arms again and lifted her into the boat. He soon placed Miss Braunschweig inside, and then Lord Braunschweig and Callum entered. Sailors followed them.

They were not trying to save the ship. There was not going to be a ship to save much longer.

The boat was dropped into the ocean with a large plop that sent additional salt water spraying over them.

This beautiful ship would be destroyed. Would all the sailors be able to save themselves? Was there even land anywhere near here? If this ship couldn't survive, how could a mere boat?

She surveyed her surroundings. Tall rocks rose through the waves like icebergs, illuminated by the bright beams of a light house. The rocks' jagged tips pointed ominously into the air, like dozens of knives, each one uniquely shaped and dangerous.

"Quick," Callum said, moving closer. He grabbed an oar and scooted beside a sailor and began rowing to assist.

At first, she didn't realize his sudden fear. But then sizzling sounded, and a great light burst through the air.

"Quick lads!" Sailors shouted and sloshed their oars through the water, looking determined.

Amber flames flew into the water, and the air burned her throat. The rocks jutted perilously close to them.

This is it.

Charlotte braced for death, but in the next moment, one of the sailors flung a rope to the shore.

We're safe.

The rope drifted back, and the sailor swore. The boat jutted away from the intended point, and drifted toward the rocks. She glanced at Callum. His face was steely, and he scanned the horizon carefully, despite his exertions in rowing.

"*Mein Gott*," Lord Braunschweig shouted, and Miss Braunschweig squeezed Charlotte's hand.

Callum was with the sailors. He had not even asked for permission. He'd seen a way in which he could help them, and he'd done so, perhaps not wanting them to offer polite excuses. It wouldn't do for any of them to ponder the fact that his station was so far above theirs.

A crowd of people stood on the rocks. They shouted and waved, and even though they were on a swirling ocean, even though the mighty ship on which they'd sailed was sinking, and even though the rocks between the boat and the people were dangerous...hope surged through her.

The sailor continued to try throwing the rope to the land, and finally, despite the wind, one of the people on the land caught it. The townspeople worked to pull their boat toward the land.

At last, the boat touched the shore, and relief soared through her.

"Come, let's go on the land." Callum extended his hand to her.

Heavens. He sounded so content, happy to not be on that swirling ship anymore.

She extended her hand to him and despised the way the mere touch of his skin, unhampered now by the barriers of gloves, sent butterflies flurrying through her body, as if she'd turned into some insect arboretum.

"Dreadful journey," Lord Braunschweig said, jumping from the ship.

Callum helped Charlotte and Miss Braunschweig onto the shore. People surged about them.

"You poor thing!" A friendly woman said, tearing off her own shawl, and wrapping Charlotte in it. "You must get yourself dry."

"Th-thank you," she stammered.

She moved over the land, following the woman, Callum at her side.

"It's a miracle you've survived dear." You wouldn't believe the number of bodies that show up here. It's a difficult corner to turn, and with that thunderstorm..." She shook her head. "The dear captain didn't stand a chance."

Charlotte looked back toward the ship.

There was nothing where it had been, only some flames floating through the water that had not yet been extinguished by the salty sea and the rain's continuous downward tumble. More boats were in the water.

"Is there a place we can stay?" Callum asked.

"There's an inn. We don't usually get guests at this time. I reckon the innkeeper has been preparing rooms for you. Are you hungry?"

Charlotte shook her head.

"I think sleep would be best for her," Callum said.

"An understanding husband," the woman declared. "I reckon you've seen worse in the war."

Callum nodded but his face still seemed stiff.

"I'm going to help the sailors," he said. "I'm going to entrust you to Lord Braunschweig and his sister. Unless you need me..."

The man was so brave. So willing to help.

She shook her head. "Stay. I'll be fine."

"I know." He nodded grimly and then gave instructions to the baron and his sister.

A thought assailed her. *I'm alive.*

She shouldn't be alive.

The storm had shattered huge sections of the ship, spraying splinters through the walls and creating jagged edges that threatened to turn into portals for the sea to rush into.

The world had seemed to topple and swerve around her for hours, tossing her about with no constraints.

The doctor had said her heart would give out were it exposed to stress. Heavens, her heart had been hammered with the fear of survival.

And yet—I'm alive.

She should be dead. The duke had married her out of pity and some short term convenience to himself. The man didn't want to be saddled with a wife, not the real kind, the kind who didn't die three months after the honeymoon.

She swallowed hard.

She couldn't meet the duke's eyes. He would realize what had happened.

Perhaps he didn't realize yet, perhaps he had some joy he didn't have to worry about burial procedures just yet, but he'd realize what had happened soon

If this stress hadn't caused her heart to give out, what would?

His jaw was set, and she wasn't sure whether the ashen pallor on the man's face was because he was assessing the prospects for them to survive this, or if he'd just determined that she was fully capable of surviving much more than this.

Chapter Twenty

"I AM WET AND VERY COLD," Lord Braunschweig grumbled. "This inn is very far from the shore."

"It seems to be close to the beach," his sister said, gazing at a half-timbered structure.

"Then the captain sank the ship in the wrong location," the baron said. "A German would have more sense."

Miss Braunschweig sent an apologetic look to Charlotte. Lord Braunschweig continued his complaints when they arrived at the inn.

"I demand to go to London at once," Lord Braunschweig said. "The farther from the ocean, the better."

"Then perhaps we should visit Oxford," Miss Braunschweig said.

Her brother narrowed his eyes. "That is most unamusing. London will suit us."

"There's a coach that stops here in the morning," the innkeeper said. "It leaves very early in the morning though."

"If I can manage a shipwreck, I can manage an early morning coach," Lord Braunschweig declared.

Charlotte was grateful when the innkeeper showed her to her room, but the sight of a soft bed and privacy did not bring joy.

She wasn't dying.

The realization should have been wonderful, the sort of announcement accompanied by full symphonies, but now horror moved through her.

Callum had married her.

Dear, sweet, lovely Callum had married her, expecting her to die before Christmas. He'd chosen her over all the other debutantes, expressly because she was ill suited to be his wife.

And now she would live.

And he had ruined his life.

Charlotte knew how cruel the *ton* could be. She knew what would happen the first time they entered a ball. She knew about all the titters and stares he would encounter, and she didn't want to live with him when he realized his act of spontaneous nobility had doomed even to a life without joy or satisfaction.

She needed to break things off between them. She needed to free him from his noble impulses. It might destroy her, but she would do it.

And Callum, dear Lord, would never suggest they part. He'd made a promise, and he was the type to honor it. He would do it, and he would never tell her he minded doing it.

But she knew Callum had never wanted to marry. If he had, he could have married Lady Isla long ago. Even if Callum tolerated her, even if she'd allowed herself to imagine he more than tolerated her, marriage would never have been the path he would have chosen.

Callum was adventurous. Now that the war was over, the man could go anywhere in the world he wanted to. He wasn't going to stay in the United Kingdom with a wife. He wasn't going to go to balls with his wife, watching as all the hostesses, tittered at him for managing to marry someone as horrible as she.

She would never permit it.

I could get an annulment.

If she left now—perhaps she could save him. Perhaps she could get an annulment. They'd consummated their marriage—Charlotte paused, pondering precisely how delicious that event had been, but Charlotte could lie. She could say they hadn't. His happiness was more important than her eternal soul.

I have to leave.

She knocked on the door to Miss Braunschweig's room. Miss Braunschweig had flung a blanket around her shoulders and it managed to look as elegant as any silver-threaded shawl.

"I would like to travel to London with you," Charlotte said.

"Of course you can come with us," Miss Braunschweig said. "You must be so frightened. I suppose the duke will want to travel up later."

Charlotte smiled. "Thank you."

She didn't mention that she was running away. She would always love Callum, always miss him, but she wouldn't force him to spend the rest of her life with him.

CALLUM SMILED AS LIGHT hit his pillow, and he stretched his arms toward Charlotte. He didn't feel her, and he opened his eyes. "Sweetheart?"

He got out of the bed, wondering at the hour. He'd arrived very late last night.

Charlotte's not going to die.

It wasn't the first time that Callum had had this thought, but normally it had been generated by a desire to protect her, to make her visit every possible doctor. He'd pushed the thought away quickly each time, cognizant that hope was an imperfect antidote to science.

But she'd survived the storm, and then, she'd survived the shipwreck.

Her heart should have given out at either of those events.

The fact she'd survived... Well, it was bloody wonderful. Perhaps the doctor had misdiagnosed her. Perhaps the doctor's apprentice had made a mistake.

Happiness jolted through him, even though Charlotte didn't seem to be in the room.

Well, she couldn't be far.

He'd thought she would be distraught after the ship wreck, but she'd seemed quiet and resigned.

His Charlotte was brave. She was the very best woman in the world.

He spotted some paper on the desk and he strode toward it. Most likely it was not for him. Perhaps some other guest had left it. But he recognized Charlotte's handwriting, and relief moved through him. Likely, she had simply gone off somewhere. Flower picking or some such thing for which she'd judged that his presence would be unnecessary.

My dearest Callum,

It seems the doctor's diagnosis was incorrect. I am alive, and as we both know, I shouldn't be after the intensity of last night.

I am returning to London with Lord Braunschweig and his sister.

Thank you for taking such good care of me. I will ensure we get an annulment.

Yours,

Charlotte

Callum's eyes widened. He reread the letter, as if he'd somehow managed to replace key words in his mind.

But the letter was absolutely the same.

She was still leaving him.

He swallowed hard, and his heartbeat throbbed in his chest.

It's impossible.

They'd just made love. They should be rejoicing. They were safe from the storm, and if her health was better—

He pulled on his clothes quickly, cursing the many buttons, all seemingly designed to keep valets in business.

She couldn't have gotten far. He would go after her. He would catch her.

His feet padded down the stairs of the inn, past the startled innkeeper. He rushed outside, and his boots sank more into the soil, muddy from last night's storm. Some birds began chirping, beginning ballads to their loved ones.

"Charlotte!" he bellowed. His voice cut through the air and seemed to echo.

There was no answer.

CHARLOTTE SAID GOODBYE to the baron and his sister and stepped into the hack they'd found for her.

"Where to miss?" the hack driver asked.

Charlotte didn't hesitate. Her family might be living in Mayfair, but there was someone else she needed to see at once. "Saint James Square."

"Very well." The driver nodded, but didn't leave.

"Take me there now," she said.

"No one is coming?" the driver asked.

"No."

The driver's eyes widened, but he started driving. Her heart quickened as she spotted the familiar ivory facades.

This was London.

She'd made it.

The hack stopped before the doctor's office. She paid the driver to wait and marched up the pavement and entered the building. The doctor's apprentice sat inside, and he rose.

"Is the doctor back from Edinburgh?" she asked.

The apprentice nodded. "Indeed. He's in his office. If you'll just wait—"

Charlotte strode past him. Niceties were things of the past.

The doctor lowered his pince-nez. "Young lady, what are you doing here?"

Charlotte squared her shoulders. She clutched the original diagnosis she'd taken from the doctor's apprentice.

"What are you doing with that scraggly piece of paper?"

Charlotte didn't flush. The doctor was right. The paper was scraggly. She'd read and reread it so many times.

"You saw me last month," she said.

"Did I?" The doctor shrugged. "I'm afraid you'll still need an appointment."

"You don't even remember me?" Charlotte asked.

"I'm sure I do," the doctor said, still staring. "Yes, yes. Of course."

"What was it that ailed me?" Charlotte asked.

"Er—you had a cold."

"I didn't," Charlotte said.

The doctor threw up his arms. "You can't expect me to remember everything."

"Perhaps then you'll remember this note you left in my file." Charlotte handed him the paper.

The man picked it up distastefully, and Charlotte tried to remind herself that a fear of infection was likely a good sign in a doctor.

"You told me that I was going to die," she said.

The man's eyebrows rose. "Did I? That can't be right."

"Read the letter."

"And you're Charlotte Butterworth?"

She nodded. "It's a unique name."

"My, my." The doctor lifted his head from the paper. "That is a mistake."

"Quite," Charlotte said.

"I hope you didn't do anything drastic about it."

She gave a tight smile. She wasn't certain whether doing something drastic entailed having a duke propose to marry her out of a mixture of sympathy and convenience, and then fleeing to the Channel Islands when the man's brother quite reasonably disapproved of the match.

And now she would have to deal with the consequences. The only thing worse than a spinster was a woman who had been married.

"Let me see," the doctor said. "I wrote that for another woman."

Charlotte felt a pang of sadness for the woman. But it made sense. The doctor was more likely to have made a mistake in addressing the letter than in conjuring up an utterly wrong diagnosis.

"She's lived a full life," the doctor said. "She's quite old. Quite old indeed. As for you... Let me see if I can find your letter in her file." He rummaged through his desk, and then he pulled up a thin folder. "Ah, yes. You have anxiety."

"A-anxiety?" Charlotte stammered.

"It's quite harmless," the doctor said.

"My chest was hurting."

"It's an experience that can affect younger women. Particularly the unmarried ones."

"Oh." Charlotte blinked.

"I suggest you don't tighten your corset too much."

"I hardly do at all," Charlotte said.

"Good," the doctor said. "Now if you can excuse me, I have work to do."

Charlotte frowned. "You should know that your misdiagnosis did affect me."

"Oh, quite, quite."

"I know it's too late for you to do anything about it, but I do want you to know that it mattered."

The doctor's face reddened. "I am a busy man, and I was preparing for a conference—"

"Take more care in the future," Charlotte said.

She rose and strode from the office. She held her head high. She'd done what she'd come to do.

Chapter Twenty-one

CALLUM HAD HOPED TO see Charlotte when he entered his London townhouse.

He certainly had not expected to see a man of similar height and exact age to himself.

"H-hamish?" he stammered.

"Callum?" Hamish raised his head from a book.

Callum frowned. Most people if they entered homes that did not belong to them did not occupy themselves with books. They preferred to hide. Or leave.

"What are you doing here?" Callum asked.

"Ah." A ruddy flush darkened Hamish's cheeks.

Callum frowned. He hadn't known his brother to have a tendency to blush.

He leveled his gaze at him.

His brother scratched the back of his neck.

"I didn't expect to see you," Hamish said finally. "It's quite nice."

"Er—yes." Callum supposed it *was* nice. "Did you develop a passion for London on your visit?"

It was the sort of thing a more sociable person than his brother might do.

"In a manner," Hamish said.

"A manner?" Callum narrowed his eyes.

Hamish's chin jutted out. "I'm staying here until I can find my own lodging in London."

"You want to *live* in London?" Callum sputtered.

"It's not so odd," Hamish said. "You've seemed to always like it."

"That's true," Callum said, wondering whether he actually had liked it, or if he'd just wanted an excuse to be far from the setting of his childhood. He suspected the latter might be the case. His two weeks in Guernsey had far exceeded any pleasures he'd ever experienced in London. He hadn't missed the theatre or ballet a single moment the entire time.

"But you've always abhorred London," Callum reminded him.

Hamish smiled. "You're right."

Callum had learned that when his brother smiled, it normally had something to do with some nefarious plot against himself.

He gazed warily around the room. The last time he'd been in a parlor alone with Hamish, dreadful things had occurred.

"I'm married," Hamish said. "I thought a London townhouse would be suitable, given that she has relatives and friends nearby. I can't expect her to change her entire life for me."

Callum's eyes widened. Hamish wouldn't marry. And if he did, he certainly wouldn't get a London townhouse. The Hamish he knew would have thought his bride would be far better removed from the Grecian facades in London which he railed against with a passion that could only belong to an architect who subscribed to a different design philosophy.

But would he marry someone whom Callum had not even met?

Callum swallowed hard.

Perhaps they truly had grown that far apart.

Callum had been so focused on protecting Hamish from Lord McIntyre's deeds that he'd stopped confiding in him completely. He'd joined the war with barely a thought about Hamish, spurred on by dreams of glory, of vindicating himself from Lord McIntyre's accusations. And now Hamish had married.

He glanced around the room, grateful they were in a drawing room and there was a variety of seats into which to collapse. He settled on the nearest one. "You never mentioned you were courting someone."

"It was a quick match."

"I see." Callum sighed. His brother had never been apt to actions of spontaneity before, but he'd decided to exercise his first one to marry someone Callum had never met.

"I think I remember you didn't invite me to the wedding," Hamish said.

"Yes," Callum said.

There had seemed to be a good reason to do that, but now he was reminded only that Hamish was his brother and the only relative still alive.

"Besides," Hamish said. "I know you'll approve."

"Oh?" Callum said, casting his mind on if he'd ever encouraged Hamish to make a match with a particular woman. Whom would Hamish think suitable?

A horrible thought struck him.

Hamish always prided himself on his honor, a virtue that seemed forever compelling him to do unpleasant tasks.

Hamish wouldn't have taken it upon himself to marry Lady Isla? The woman he'd grown up assuming Callum would marry?

Callum's heart beat an uncomfortable rhythm.

"You shouldn't look so horrified at the thought of my marriage," Hamish said. "I thought you would be pleased."

"Pleased?" Callum's voice was hoarse, and he coughed.

"Naturally," Hamish said. "Your engagement seemed inexplicable, and mine—"

Hamish's eyes sparkled, and Callum blinked.

Hamish's eyes didn't sparkle. Not for years at least. They glowered on occasion, and they were quite adept at narrowing so they seemed to bore into whomever Hamish spoke to, but they never sparkled. Was it possible Hamish was in love?

The thought seemed absurd, more even than happening upon Hamish here.

And yet... Callum gazed at his twin brother again. Hamish's lips could hardly be described as veering downward.

"Are you happy?" Callum asked tentatively.

"Oh, indeed." Hamish grinned. "She's wonderful, Callum. She's marvelous. Divine."

"Divine?" Callum blinked.

"Utterly," Hamish breathed and leaned back into the sofa cushions.

"That's splendid," Callum said.

"Now where's your wife?" Hamish said. "I know mine is eager to see her."

Callum's smile wobbled. "You still haven't told me who your wife is."

Hamish's eyes widened. "I thought it was obvious. It's Georgiana."

Georgiana.

"You married the elder Miss Butterworth?"

"Your wife's sister." Hamish grinned. "Two sisters married two brothers. Quite nice, don't you think? It will make holidays ever so practical."

A pain moved through Callum. He didn't want to admit that Charlotte had run away from him. He'd tried to give her everything, and at the first sign of good health, she'd bolted.

He covered his face in his hands.

"Callum?" Hamish's voice was filled with a sympathy Callum did not associate with him. Evidently married life had changed him.

"She's gone," Callum said.

"I don't understand," Hamish said.

The statement was baffling. Wives weren't supposed to flee. Women weren't supposed to even travel by themselves, much less decide to make a new life.

"I suppose you had a bit of a tiff."

"It was no tiff." Callum almost laughed. Bits of tiffs were generally supposed to be about different tastes in household decor. Bits of tiffs certainly did not describe Charlotte's actions.

The thing was... They hadn't even argued. There'd been no sign she was unhappy. If there had been...He would have rectified it. Instead he only had her note.

In which she distinctly expressed the fact that she didn't want to see him again.

Callum rose. "She doesn't want me to be here."

Hamish widened his eyes. "I suppose it's because you've been married longer than Georgiana and I."

"What do you mean?"

"Only that it's understandable you would have had your first argument before us. Chronologically it makes sense. Logically too."

Callum gave his brother a tentative smile. "Just why are you married to Charlotte's sister? I seem to remember you heading off to Scotland."

Hamish smiled. "It's a long story."

"You despised her."

"I hardly knew her."

"That didn't stop you from criticizing her."

"I was a fool," Hamish said. "And now—"

"—You're buying a home in London."

"We don't have our castle anymore," Hamish said. "After your marriage—"

Oh.

"I told you that you shouldn't move out."

"The mortgage belongs to the McIntyre family. Duty—"

"—Blast duty," Callum said, and Hamish blinked. "You should have told me."

Hamish was supposed to stay in their home. Lord McIntyre wasn't supposed to secure a brilliant home for his descendants. Not if the method of securing the home had involved murder and deceit.

Callum paced the room. He had to fix this.

He swung around. "I'm getting that castle back."

"Now?" Hamish stammered.

"Naturally not," Callum said. "First I have to get my wife back."

CHARLOTTE KNOCKED ON the door of her parents' townhouse, wrapping her cloak tightly around her. The door swung open, and Flora stood before her. The maid widened her eyes, and Charlotte darted inside quickly.

It seemed odd that everything would look the same. She was quite certain it was supposed to be different. Everything in the world had changed. She'd eloped and lived the life briefly, albeit blissfully, as a married woman.

But the same thin Persian carpet was on the floor, and the same small mirror hung over the same sideboard.

"Are my parents in?" Charlotte asked.

Flora nodded rapidly. "They arrived back recently. They're in the drawing room."

"Good," Charlotte said, even though good wasn't quite the appropriate word when one was about to forever disappoint one's parents.

This was the moment she'd been dreading. No crater in the road surpassed this in discomfort.

"Darling!" Her mother's voice sailed through the drawing room and into the entrance. Footsteps quickly followed, and soon the door swung open, slamming against the sideboard, and her mother strode out, the ribbons on her cap bouncing from the recent expulsion of energy. "It's you!"

"Yes," Charlotte said, but her mother narrowed the distance between them and crushed her against her chest before

Charlotte could stammer further confirmation of her existence.

"And where is my son?" Mama jerked her head in the direction of the door.

The closed door.

The door that was not going to open anytime soon, and certainly not to reveal the duke.

Charlotte swallowed hard. "He's not here."

"Well, obviously not, my dear," Mama said. "But when is he arriving?"

The tension in Charlotte's body soared. Speaking might be something she'd long ago mastered, but at the moment the exact process seemed complex and unwieldy. Her tongue was too thick, and her throat too dry to attempt to speak properly.

Mama glanced at the door, and she relaxed her features, prepared to smile at her son-in-law.

Mama had always been fond of the duke, satisfied of his good intentions even as the rest of London seemed to whisper at the suddenness of his engagement, whispering whether she might have found herself impregnated by him, though the fact he had chosen her of all women to bed seemed to befuddle them.

Footsteps padded through the room.

Papa.

Relief at seeing him, relief she was no longer traveling by herself, fought with her shame.

Georgiana would understand, and she headed upstairs.

"Where are you going?" Mama called.

"I'm going to see my sister."

"You have been gone for very long," Mama said.

"Y-yes." Charlotte paused. "Is she not here?" She turned toward the window. The rain was quite strong.

It was unlikely Georgiana had decided to go to Hyde Park in this weather, but perhaps she was calling on someone.

"Georgiana doesn't live here anymore," Mama announced.

"Excuse me?"

There was no reason for Georgiana to not live at home. Where else could she go? Was she visiting one of Mama's relatives? The thought was odd. Georgiana got on well with their parents, particularly Papa. There was no reason why she would want to go to some far off place, unless—

No.

She couldn't be married.

There was no one whom Georgiana would marry, was there? Georgiana was a wallflower. She didn't have any prospects. Men were wary of her red hair, and the supposed poor qualities that went along with it and could be passed on to children. If people took on a less medieval opinion on redheads and inquired about her, they would be informed about her poor position.

That's why Charlotte had desired to marry Callum. She'd known that Georgiana had no prospects, and she'd wanted to give her parents some bliss.

"I don't understand," Charlotte said.

Unless—

Her shoulders sank. "She didn't marry the curate?"

The curate had been Georgiana's one caller. He'd been a nice enough person, but hardly equal to her sister. His prospects would lead to an even lower standard of living than Papa's.

"Oh, no. She's not married to a duke, of course, but I assure you, she is *very* well married." Mama gave a secretive sort of smile.

"Whom did she marry?" Charlotte asked.

"You must know!"

"I don't," Charlotte said.

"Oh, dear. The mail must be horrid in Guernsey. Well, she married your husband's brother of course."

"Of course?" Charlotte's eyes widened.

There was nothing natural about that occurrence. Georgiana had been very wary of Hamish. She'd warned Charlotte against him, and had even openly argued with him after Hamish had admittedly been quite inappropriate.

But Hamish had seemed to give no indication that he would want to marry Georgiana. He'd seemed sufficiently disapproving of Charlotte, and she'd seen no indication that he would have wanted to tie his life with her older sister.

"It's possible Georgiana is in your husband's townhouse," Mama said. "Perhaps they'll all visit together."

Charlotte flinched. Now was the moment to tell them. Now was the moment to say that the marriage they had been so proud of, was nothing like what they'd thought.

"He's not coming," she said.

"I expect he has much to do at that club."

"I expect he has much to do too, but he's not coming. Here."

"You mean he's dead?" Papa widened his eyes, and his fingers moved to his forehead.

Papa was a vicar, and he was no doubt likely to quote some Biblical passage. But it wasn't necessary. Callum was very much alive—just not with her.

Charlotte shook her head. "We should never have gotten married. It was all a lie."

"But you did elope in Guernsey?" Papa said sternly. "He didn't run off with you and then not marry you?"

"No, no, no," Charlotte said quickly. "He is a man of honor. I'm afraid he's not ever arriving."

"Was he taken ill?" Mama clutched her hand to her chest. "That poor sweet boy. It was food poisoning, wasn't it? The man seemed quite uneasy at what his brother slipped into the tea. Most naughty of his twin. And heavens, you were in the Channel Islands! Think of the possibility for food poisonings! All that fish. So many varieties. And how many are venomous?"

"We did not encounter any," Charlotte said. "He does not suffer from food poisoning." She paused. She hadn't seen Callum in days. "At least, he does not suffer from food poisoning that I know about."

"Then he's still alive?" Mama asked sharply.

Charlotte nodded. "I would assume. The man is in good health, and statistically he should still be alive.

Her cheeks flamed as she considered how easily she'd been persuaded to believe that her health was poor.

"In fact I left him."

"You left a duke?" Mama's voice wobbled.

"I did," Charlotte said miserably.

"And people call me the unsensible one in the family," Mama huffed. "Am I to understand you traveled here by yourself?"

"I took a mailing coach with...friends," Charlotte said. "I know it must seem undignified."

"Undignified?" Mama exclaimed. "It is utterly unlike you. It is difficult enough to persuade you to attend a ball. Guernsey must have changed you."

Charlotte blinked.

Mama was correct.

She would never have ventured on her own otherwise. The fact she had changed in Guernsey due to the duke's influence only steadied her resolve.

Voices ushered through the door accompanied by the definite sound of *banging*.

Charlotte frowned. No one was in the habit of banging on the front door. Papa was a vicar, and hardly in the habit of going about upsetting people, and even the most stringent parishioners were unlikely to desire to see Papa urgently for their eternal salvation. They were hardly Catholics.

"Charlotte! Charlotte!" Callum's pleasant tenor voice barreled through the thick door. The pitch he'd chosen might not be the most elegant, but it still sent a rush of longing through her. The rough sound had an air of desperation entirely uncalled for.

Callum wasn't supposed to be here.

Flora dashed toward the door.

"You don't have to open that," Charlotte called out.

"Of course she has to," Mama said. "It's your husband. And my son."

Mama rushed to the hallway, as if there was a possibility Flora might not open the door. Charlotte stood up and darted her gaze about the tiny room. If only she could leave.

She couldn't face Callum.

The man would be honorable and state things he didn't mean, things she wanted so badly to believe.

No.

She had to leave. She ran toward the window. If only people in past decades had thought to make windows larger. She glanced at the door, but thankfully no one had entered. *Yet.*

She took a deep sigh, drew the curtains, pushed the window pane open, placed her knee on the ledge and ducked her head through the opening and—

"Charlotte!" Her mother's voice soared through the room. "Are you climbing *out* the window?"

Her mother's surprise and disapproval was evident.

"I—er—" She glanced around, and her mother's eyebrow arched upward. "The door functions quite well."

"Charlotte?" Concern emanated through Callum's voice. The man's eyes were round.

No disapproval was in it, just worry.

He's sorry for me.

The man had always been. He'd been concerned when he'd thought she was dying, and even now that he did not think she was bound to spontaneously collapse and be placed into a coffin, he still thought her so awkward, so lacking in the grace common in most debutantes, that he continued to feel sympathy for her.

Her cheeks flamed, and heat pricked the back of her neck. She removed her foot from the ledge and hastily placed it on the floor.

"Darling!" Callum said.

She tried to smile, but her lips wobbled.

"I'm not—not *that* anymore." She stopped. Reminding him they were no longer together was hard. It went against everything she most desired.

His face sobered, and he dropped hold of her hands. Her heart ached, but his gaze didn't leave her face.

"Forgive me," he said.

Her heart ached further. "You have nothing to ask my forgiveness for."

"Sweetheart," Callum said. "I want you to be by my side. Forever."

She shook her head. "You don't mean that."

"I do. We're married."

She smiled sadly. "I'm—I'm so sorry about this. Forgive me."

"You love me," Callum said.

She blinked. "That's a pompous thing to say."

"Did you only tell me that because of the storm?"

She swooped her eyelashes downward. She was sure she had been taught some rules of eloquence, but clearly nothing had lingered.

"I hope you love me," Callum continued, "Because I bloody well love you."

She blinked.

He sighed. "And perhaps I should apologize for swearing—but honestly, that's the least of my concerns."

"What's your main concern?"

"Trying to get you to see that I want to live with you... Forever and ever."

"No." She firmed her jaw.

Something gnawed at her heart, but she stayed firm. "I didn't mean to manipulate you. I didn't mean to do any of that," she said. "But clearly I did. And I won't let you ruin all your wonderful plans by marrying me."

"You think I can't include you in my life?"

"You're a rogue. You have needs, I understand."

He scrutinized her. "You would do that for me?"

"Naturally."

Callum smiled. Most likely, the man thought that Charlotte would succumb. How could she resist him? It wasn't just that he was incredibly handsome. It wasn't just that he was a duke. No, he was kind and wonderful.

But it was for that reason that she couldn't accept his plea.

"YOU MUST LEAVE." CHARLOTTE'S expression was cold.

Charlotte's expression wasn't supposed to be cold.

Not now.

Not now that they'd grown to know one another.

Her demeanor was as stiff and uncertain as when they'd first met.

But then he was fairly certain he wasn't supposed to be at a loss for words. That hadn't been an affliction which he'd ever suffered from.

"How lovely to see you both married." Mrs. Butterworth beamed, darting her eyes from Callum to Charlotte with evident delight. "It's so romantic. You had a tiff, and now here he is again, begging you to return to him."

"Then you'll say yes?" His voice quivered.

"I should have known that you would come after me. I am afraid I must apologize to you."

"No need to, sweetheart," he said.

She stiffened at the sound of his pet name.

"I must apologize, because I am afraid you have journeyed a great deal for no purpose."

"No purpose?" His eyes widened.

She reflected. "Perhaps you will be able to see to your business at Hades' Lair."

"That's not why I came here."

"You came to see me," she said. "Because you are good and honorable and magnificent.

But I cannot return to you."

"Charlotte Eliza Butterworth!" her mother screamed. "What do you think you're doing?"

"Setting him free."

"But he's your husband!"

"Dukes are known for debauchery. Perhaps he can get an annulment. Perhaps Papa can say the man absconded without his consent—"

"Absolutely not," Papa said. "That man is your husband."

"He shouldn't be tied to me for the rest of my life. It would be unfair." Tears flooded her eyes, and she rushed upstairs.

Chapter Twenty-two

CALLUM STRODE OVER the familiar plush carpet of Hades' Lair. Crystal chandeliers, obtained from Murano, glimmered in their familiar fashion, aided by the newly lit twelve hour candles. Raucous laughter sounded from the next room. The night was still beginning; the guests could still cherish dreams of brandishing buckets of coin. Alcohol would buoy on that illusion for longer than the guests might otherwise be victim to.

The air seemed thick, as if smoke still wafted from the patrons' cigars. The red leather chairs were empty. At some point, the club would fill again, but now it was afternoon.

"Ah, you're back," Sir Seymour said. "The club isn't the same without you."

Callum slowed his pace and gave his best attempt at a smile.

Now he was in public again. Now he had to be proper.

The action of smiling seemed all together unfamiliar, and his lips felt tight. Charlotte had shattered his heart. Sir Seymour, though, gave no indication of anything being amiss, and his smile did not falter.

"Most dull without you. I must let you know there have been the most atrocious rumors about you."

"Oh?" Callum didn't bother to raise a brow. His reputation was hardly an issue of concern.

"Oh, indeed." Sir Seymour beamed. "Most distressing. In fact, I do rather despise sharing the information with you. Still, I feel it is my duty, as a frequent visitor of Hades' Lair, to inform you that people are saying you're off in the Channel Islands. With the second daughter of someone in the cloth."

"Are they?" Callum asked. He leveled his eyes at Sir Seymour. "Her mother used to be friends with your wife."

"A fact we prefer not to talk about," Sir Seymour said. "The earl will be most happy to see you. He has been asking about you often."

Wolfe is here.

Callum's heart tumbled down farther.

"I will see him now," Callum said.

"Quite right." Sir Seymour hesitated. "If you have a pistol, I suggest you bring it."

Callum braced himself and headed toward Wolfe's suite. Earlier he might have run away, escaping to the arbory fortifications of Hyde Park, but this time he didn't hesitate to enter.

A fast-tempo music filled the air, and Callum ignored the queasy feeling of his stomach.

Other people played the piano well, and the club even employed an excellent pianist, but no one could approach the keys with such unrestrained gayety. The order of notes made no difference to him. High and low notes could exist together.

Normally Callum felt a sliver of pride on Wolfe's behalf. The man had struggled to read as a child, and his intelligence had been doubted. Perhaps that had been why Wolfe's father had been so eager to become the guardian of Callum and his brother, and so eager to arrange a marriage between Callum and his only daughter.

Once Wolfe had a tutor who'd succumbed to his frequent demands to be taught the piano, and Wolfe's skill had become evident, no one had doubted the man's intelligence any longer and found him in any manner lacking.

Callum frowned. He'd imagined this would be his moment of triumph. Sir Seymour had said that Wolfe was upset, and now he could gloat.

And yet the only emotion he felt was disgust at himself.

He was filled with unhappiness. How could he wish it on anyone else?

Wolfe glanced up.

"Callum! You look terrible." Wolfe arched his eyebrows and poured whiskey into a crystal tumbler. He placed the whiskey on the table before Callum.

Callum eyed the amaretto-colored drink. Charlotte was well, was expected to live long, but she'd decided to spend her life without him. No drink would distract him from that, and he pushed it away.

"You've had more polite days," Wolfe said.

"I've also had more happy days," Callum grumbled.

"And you could have had more if you'd only married my sister," Wolfe said. "What on earth were you thinking? Charlotte Butterworth? Hardly a suitable match for a duke."

"You don't know her."

"I know she's the daughter of a vicar. Untraveled. Quite unsuitable. Just because women aren't supposed to work does not mean they have to be devoid of any qualities."

"You don't know Miss Charlotte Butterworth at all."

"You're being terribly testy about her."

"I am married to her."

Wolfe scanned him, and Callum shivered under the intensity of the man's gaze. "The experience does not seem to have benefited you."

"That's not true," Callum said.

Charlotte *had* changed him. He'd been cold, callous before.

"I'm sorry about your sister," Callum said.

"It's not me you should apologize to," Wolfe said.

Callum nodded. He knew. "Has she returned to London?"

Wolfe gave a short laugh. "Unfortunately so. She arrived from a country house party to the dreadful news."

"I hope she wasn't too offended."

"At having the man she was betrothed to marry another woman? And one so beneath her?" Wolfe gave a wry laugh.

"I'm so sorry."

Wolfe jerked his head toward Callum. "Don't pity her. She'll be fine. Just stay away from her."

Callum nodded, conscious his stomach felt queasy even though he hadn't taken a single sip of Wolfe's whisky.

"How is the marriage?"

"She wants an annulment," Callum said miserably.

Wolfe chuckled. "That didn't work for Henry the Eighth."

"She hasn't been married to me for a decade."

"Annulments are never granted," Wolfe said.

"She's prepared to say the marriage was never consummated."

"That doesn't sound like you," Wolfe said.

Callum flushed. He'd tried so hard to be virtuous.

Wolfe stared at him. "Then again, you are a duke. Perhaps the current Archbishop of Canterbury will be easier to convince than the one in Henry the Eighths time."

"I don't desire an annulment," Callum said.

"You mean to say you have fallen for her? Miss Charlotte Butterworth? Second daughter to a vicar?" Wolfe chuckled.

"She's the most wonderful woman in the world," Callum said.

Wolfe chuckled again.

"We need to talk about Montgomery Castle," Callum said.

"Oh?"

"Your father was dishonest," Callum said.

The grin on Wolfe's face vanished, and Callum told Wolfe about the ledgers, about Lord McIntyre's words to him and about his own suspicions about his aunt's death. Charlotte might not want anything to do with him, but it was she who had given him strength. He didn't need to live in Montgomery Castle, but he would no longer permit anyone to demean his parents' memory and he would no longer allow the McIntyre family to profit off of his parents' demise.

Wolfe tapped his fingers against his desk. "I received a curious letter from a solicitor a week ago stating something similar."

Callum blinked, and Wolfe smoothed out a letter. "The solicitor seems to have been hired by your wife, and it mentions some ledgers that he has in his possession."

"Indeed?" Callum felt his eyes widen. He'd assumed the ledgers had been lost in the shipwreck.

Wolfe gave him a small smile. "Perhaps she does not desire to remain married to you, but it seems that she was already working to get your estate back. She must have hired quite a clever accountant, but the facts seem clear. I am afraid my father may have misled you and I—er—apologize."

Callum bowed his head. "Thank you."

He'd assumed the books had been lost in the shipwreck. It seemed that Charlotte had been working even harder on the project than he expected and had already given them to someone else.

"I expect you will want to return to your estate now. I can't pay you all the money our father stole from you, but I can give you that."

"I think I might want to sell it," Callum admitted. "There are too many memories there."

"I see." Wolfe shrugged. "I might be able to help you with that."

"So you're not going to fight the claim?" Callum asked.

"I might run a gaming hell, but that doesn't mean the concept of honor is foreign to me."

Callum nodded. Wolfe had fought heroically in France.

"You're a bastard for breaking off the betrothal with Isla, but you are still my best friend," Wolfe continued. "Besides, I would have a hard time fighting the case. The accountant was damned good."

"The very best," Callum said, and his chest swelled as he thought of Charlotte.

CHARLOTTE TRIED TO adjust to her new life. She still visited Hyde Park, conscious she should do her best to live her life, even without Callum. /

The pain had not dissipated, despite her best efforts.

She strolled through the park with Georgiana. Charlotte tried to find pleasure in the open sky and the feel of the wind on her face. The vast landscape seemed not quite as impressive as before. She was too conscious the park existed because of the whims of the people in London than because of nature. It was too manicured, too perfect, and she sought to dismiss the pang of longing. There was no ocean, no waves to brush against, no rocks to stroll upon, no cliffs on which to watch bright fishing boats bob up and down. Perhaps the Serpentine would be the most similar thing she would experience to Guernsey.

The temperature was higher, and the birds seemed to chirp with rather more vigor than normal, as if optimistic of their chances of drawing a mate.

Hopefully they could be fortunate.

Charlotte knew now the reason so many women pressed marriage on others was not merely so they would not be a bother on parents who would no longer need to provide for her, but because a good marriage was something to aspire to, even if in reality it was something quite rare. Still, her parents had managed to find it, as had, more surprisingly, her sister Georgiana. She was happy for Georgiana, even if it meant she could never entirely forget about Callum.

She would always be conscious if her parents went to Scotland for Christmas, wondering if Callum was there, or if he would rush off to some corner in Europe, pretending to take a sudden interest in French art or Italian wine, when everyone knew it was really just to avoid her.

The trees were no longer pink and lilac. The blossoms had long ago been replaced with thick green leaves that clung firmly to the trees. This was England at its very finest. This was happiness. She knew that. Everyone around her was happy. Every other person was smiling, beaming into the sky as if the only thing they needed was the sun hundreds and hundreds and hundreds of miles above them. *I'm happy,* she said to herself, but even in her own thoughts, it felt like a lie.

She might be alive, she might have her life granted and yet she was for some ridiculous reason discontent. Those blissful months with Callum in Guernsey had changed everything. She sighed. It didn't matter. It didn't matter what she thought. The important thing was that Callum was free.

Georgiana stiffened. "Don't look to the right."

"Why not?"

"It's someone unpleasant," Georgiana said.

"Oh."

"Ah. Charlotte Butterworth," a familiar voice said that caused ice to invade Charlotte's heart. "Or should I say Your Grace?"

Charlotte swallowed hard and turned to see Lady Isla.

"Forgive me," Lady Isla said, in a confident tone. "Normally etiquette does not elude *me,* but your status seems unclear. Most duchesses do not live with their parents."

"I expect you don't need to call me anything," Charlotte said. "Since we are not friends."

Lady Isla frowned and her dark lashes moved over her pale icy eyes. Her steely composure seemed rather less steely. "That is beside the point."

Charlotte raised her eyebrows, and Lady Isla departed rapidly.

Georgiana stifled a laugh. Her sister leaned closer to her. "You have changed."

"I just didn't know the answer."

"Nonsense. You would never have addressed Lady Isla like that before."

"I hope I wasn't too rude. I forgot you're her neighbor."

Georgiana waved her hand dismissively. "I am sure she thought you rude, but sometimes the occasion calls for it."

Chapter Twenty-three

"YOU LOOK LOVELY," MAMA said.

"Only my best dress was available," Charlotte said.

"Indeed?" Mama asked blithely. "Oh, I did forget. Flora is doing the washing?"

"Not all my clothes needed washing."

"Oh, indeed?"

"They were in the wardrobe. But now they're gone." Charlotte narrowed her eyes.

"How very curious," Mama said. "Oh, well. I suppose there must be an explanation. Perhaps Mayfair has been beset by clothes thieves."

"A good clothes thief would take my best dress," Charlotte said.

"A good thief would take jewels. We are hardly dealing with the very best."

"I doubt we are dealing with thieves at all."

"Don't be too certain."

Charlotte frowned. Mama seemed to be acting most suspiciously.

"Are you going to the park now?" Mama asked.

"I always do at this time," Charlotte said.

"Yes," Mama beamed. "Darling, let me come with you."

"You want to ride the cart with me?"

"Of course, dear."

"You've never gone on buggy rides with me before."

"That was when I was young and foolish, darling."

"I haven't been gone that long," Charlotte muttered.

Mama gave a broad smile and glanced at her husband. "Remember not to spend too much time with Hegel today."

Papa turned the page of his book absentmindedly, as if he weren't even reading it, and his eyes sparkled.

Mama squeezed into the cart with Charlotte and Georgiana, and they left for Hyde Park. Soon Charlotte guided the horses onto Rotten Row.

Rapid horse hooves sounded behind her, and she glanced over her shoulder to see a curricle rapidly approaching.

Charlotte tightened her hands about the reins and directed the horses off the gravel and tan bridle path toward the wooden fencing that separated the path from the public walkways as the curricle rushed her.

Who was disturbing her quiet day?

"That man is driving too quickly," she murmured.

"As if he desires to crash into us," Mama said, for some reason smiling.

Charlotte stiffened, remembering the last time a man had crashed into their coach.

It couldn't be him.

He was probably at some house party in Sussex, admiring the ocean from the safety of the British borders. It would be ridiculous to glance back at the curricle, as if the driver desired to get her attention. She knew better.

And yet...

The horses from the curricle still trotted closely behind her own.

"Charlotte! Charlotte!" A distinctive male voice shouted behind her.

It couldn't be *him.*

Most likely she'd simply heard the murmurings of the wind through the trees. She remembered the sound of his voice so well—it was no wonder it was going through her head now. What other men did she know besides him?

"Perhaps we'll be run over," Mama said.

"Once there's a clearing, I will pull the cart over. We're not going to get run over, no matter how fast that driver behind us drives."

"What a good idea," Mama said.

"Oh, indeed," Georgiana said, equally unconcerned about the curricle chasing them.

Charlotte spotted a clearing and directed the horses to pull over. The whole thing was unnecessary. Why had the curricle followed so closely behind her? At least now the carriage could pass her, and she would no longer think of Callum.

Wheels and horse hooves sounded behind her, and she turned.

Shiny blond hair gleamed in the sunshine, adorned with a glossy top hat.

Callum.

The man wore a suit that would have rivalled anything in Beau Brummel's closet. His clothes weren't wrinkled, and no one could mistake him for anything else but a duke. He radiated handsomeness, and for a moment Charlotte's heart stopped.

How could she have married him? How could she have imagined a man like him had anything to do with her?

He practically glittered. In fact—given the way the sunlight was coming from the leaves, he did in fact glitter.

"Charlotte," he said.

His voice sounded husky, and he stared into her eyes.

"Oh, my." Mama fanned herself.

Charlotte swallowed hard.

"I'm happy to have found you," Callum said.

"Of course," Charlotte said.

He raised his eyebrows.

"I mean, you're speaking to me..." Her voice wobbled, and she had the impression she might have said the wrong thing again. Her chest tightened. How was she supposed to think when she was with him? Her eyes only wanted to look at him, to feast in the attractive planes of his face and the way he wore a suit so nicely.

"I am happy to see you," he said reassuringly.

"Your voice is like velvet," she said.

The man's lips twitched, and she flushed.

"You're distracting me," she said reproachfully.

He didn't laugh, but his eyes were still kind. He hopped up from his curricle.

"May I join you?" he asked.

She nodded, conscious her fingers were trembling. She moved them hastily away and folded them onto her lap.

He abandoned his curricle and approached her.

Mama cleared her throat. "You know I've always wanted to be in a curricle. Haven't you, Georgiana?"

"Oh, indeed," Georgiana said, grinning. "I want to see how a curricle works too."

"Georgiana. You should stay..."

"Nonsense," Mama said. "These reins look quite intriguing. I wonder if driving a curricle is just like driving a cart."

"But you never drive a cart, Mama," Charlotte said.

Georgian walked hastily to the curricle, and this time Charlotte did not protest. Hopefully her sister would prevent Mama from injuring herself.

The curricle moved. "I got it to work," Mama said triumphantly.

"Splendid," Callum said.

For some reason the duke didn't seem concerned about Mama and Georgiana driving off with his curricle. If something was making him nervous, it wasn't that.

Could it be just the prospect of being along with Charlotte?

She frowned. He certainly was giving every appearance of being nervous.

"Let me sit beside you." He climbed into the cart and took the reins, urging the horses into a trot.

"Where are you taking me?" she gasped.

"We've never been to Jersey yet," he murmured.

"Jersey?" Her mouth fell open.

"In the Channel Islands," he said, and the horses began to canter.

"You don't need to explain geography to me." She crossed her arms and looked sternly at him, a task which should have been more lauded than it was. All her instincts were telling her to hold onto the edge of the cart with all her might. The world swerved about her, a flurry of bright colors. The air brushed against her skin

"Perhaps we won't visit Jersey," he admitted.

"Good," she murmured, conscious of a prickle of disappointment. She pushed the feeling away.

It was good if he was becoming more sensible.

Perhaps he had only wanted to see her to assure her she'd been correct to leave him, and that he was indulging in his normal life of roguish glee with such enthusiasm he felt compelled to speak with her now, lest next time in her presence he find himself in a drunken haze and could not recognize her.

Somehow, that thought did not seem reassuring.

Still, she straightened and smoothed her dress. She wanted him to be happy. That was all. It was what the man undoubtedly deserved.

"You seem well. I'm glad," she said matter-of-factly, doing her best to quell any lingering thought that he need not seem not nearly as openly joyful.

Usually she found it quite pleasant to be correct and derived much satisfaction from solving mathematical equations, but in this case, it did not seem absolutely necessary for the man to display his joy quite so fully.

He reached over and squeezed her hand. Her nerves tingled, but she valiantly raised her chin.

"I'm sure that's not appropriate."

"It's utterly appropriate," he said smoothly. "You are my wife. And you love me."

Her cheeks flamed. "I said that in a moment of weakness."

"Are you saying it's not true?"

She was silent.

"It's fine," he said, more calmly now. "You see the thing is, I love you."

She blinked. That wasn't what the purpose of the meeting was. He was supposed to declare that she was correct and that he was thankful to her for restoring his life to him.

"You needn't be so surprised," he said. "I remember telling you before."

She swallowed hard, and her heart thudded.

"That was under the influence of the storm. Emotions can become heightened in moments of extreme anxiety. It would be wrong to hold yourself to the sudden whims of a moment of terror."

"That is quite nice of you, but I assure you I have no problem being beholden to those emotions.

The cart moved swiftly through the park. Great trees soared above them, and sunbeams cast golden light through the leaves, so the ground seemed to sparkle.

Charlotte inhaled the woodsy scent. Callum made everything more magical.

I never want to leave.

Soon though, rows of buildings stood majestically before them.

"Where are you going?" she asked.

"You'll see."

"You must tell me."

"St. George's."

It can't be.

"You have a sudden urge to be religious?"

This wasn't Sunday. There would be no service. And St. George's was the most fashionable church for weddings. It was, of course, where they had originally planned to marry.

The cart moved onto the cobblestones, and the wheels rumbled against the uneven ground. They were thrust into a whirl of gray stone buildings, albeit with elaborate facades, and Callum slowed the curricle as traffic filled the street.

Charlotte had avoided this section of London. The last time she'd been here had been riding in a carriage with her family, on the way to her wedding at St. George's. Her heart tightened.

"Is someone we know getting married?" she asked feebly.

His eyes glinted again, filled with humor. "Yes."

"Are you going to tell me more?"

"I thought you were quite good at figuring out puzzles. I'm sure you've worked it out."

Her heart thudded again.

Our wedding.

She didn't want to utter it. She didn't want to be wrong. She didn't want to admit to herself that—

She tried to force the feelings away.

The cart moved into St. George's Square, and the familiar columned church rose before them. Children were outside, armed with rose petals.

Everyone seemed to be smiling.

Some people she recognized, members of the *ton.* Louisa Carmichael was there, and her family.

"My darling Charlotte," Callum said. "Will you please do me the honor of becoming my wife?"

She blinked. "We're already married."

He grinned. "Precisely." He leaned toward her, and his scent sent a wave of yearning through her body, remembering their closeness on the ship, before their whole world collapsed about them. "Still, I thought you might value my declarations more if all of our friends and family attended."

She moved her gaze toward the church. "They're all inside?"

He shrugged. "It's quite full. I'm afraid some of the patrons from my club also insisted on coming."

"And you kept it a secret?"

"Your mother kept it a secret." Callum squeezed her hand. "Now please say yes."

"But your life... Your future..."

"...Is better with you in it," Callum said, his voice serious. "I've missed you so much."

"B-but you could have anyone," she stammered. "You're a duke. I'm sure you could convince the archbishop to give you an annulment, and there must be many women willing to overlook our previous marriage."

His lips quirked. "Though I'm happy at your belief in the strength of my powers of persuasion and charm, I don't want anyone else except about you. You make me see the world in a new way. You are perfect."

Charlotte's heart quivered.

"That doctor may have made a clerical error, but it was the very best thing he could have done, for he brought us together." Callum moved from the cart and offered her his hand. "The wedding guests are waiting."

Charlotte was silent, still taken aback.

"You will say yes?" Callum's voice wobbled, and his eyes seemed to grow rounder. "If you don't desire to marry me after all—" His voice broke up, and he swallowed hard. "I've missed you so much. But if you have found the distance between us pleasant—"

"N-no." Charlotte stammered. She couldn't let him think she didn't adore him.

"I love you. I love you more than anything." Callum raised his chin obstinately, as if willing her to argue. It seemed easy to imagine his ancestors bravely battling. All that was missing was shining armor, though the sun glinted over his tailcoat and waistcoat with such force even that was easy to envision.

Charlotte took her hand and looked at him. *Of course I love him.*

She'd whispered the words to him in the dark, but now she inhaled and uttered them aloud. Her heart trembled, conscious the words would change everything.

There'd been safety perhaps in being a bluestocking. Safety in assuming a duke would never desire to marry her. Safety in withdrawing herself from the competitive nature of other debutantes. Because some people criticized her habit of immersing herself in books, she'd assumed everyone would.

He swallowed hard, and she realized she'd been silent.

"Do you love me?" he asked again.

"I do," she said quickly. "I-I love you too. I—"

He pulled her into his arms, sweeping her easily from the cart.

"Wonderful," he said, and his lips spread into that familiar grin.

"I don't think it's proper to hold me like this."

Callum leaned toward. "Good thing you're already married."

He strode up the steps with her, still carrying her in his arms.

Children giggled and threw petals at them, and Charlotte inhaled their fragrant floral scent. How had she ever imagined weddings were not the most wonderful thing in the world? The distance to the portico was slight, but she indulged in each movement.

She wasn't dying.

She was healthy and would live longer.

But now she knew to cherish each movement.

Callum pushed open the door to the church. For one moment, she stiffened. The church was so full, so entirely unlike their hasty elopement in Guernsey and even entirely unlike the small, intimate wedding they'd planned here once before.

"But I could have said no," she whispered. "You would have been humiliated."

"That wouldn't compare to the pain of losing you," he said.

"What compelled you?"

"I may have run into Lady Isla," he admitted. "She was upset you didn't say you would no longer be called a duchess."

Charlotte smiled, conscious of the feel of Callum's arms about her.

The last time they'd been here the doors to the church had been locked, but now they opened easily.

"Ready?" Callum asked.

"For the rest of my life," Charlotte breathed.

Music started to play, and joy filled her. The day might be gray, an uncomfortable brisk breeze might be blowing, but it was still wonderful.

Epilogue

1825

Guernsey

A warm breeze brushed against Callum as white and pink blossoms descended around them. Callum watched their slow flight and urged the horses forward, conscious of the thick floral fragrance in the air.

"When will we be there?" Charles asked, and Charlotte squeezed their son's hand.

"Soon," she promised. "Very soon."

They had been going to Guernsey every year since Charles was two. Perhaps Callum had been born in the Highlands, perhaps Charlotte had been born in Norfolk, but it was here, in the middle of the English Channel that Callum had found home.

Callum was no longer involved in Hades' Lair. It had been a useful expression, mostly spurred by Wolfe's involvement in it. Even though plenty of people had asked if he would be fine moving to a more rural location, he'd found only contentment. He was happy to give his son the childhood he'd wished he'd had for longer.

"When are they coming?" Charles asked.

"Soon," Callum said. "Very soon. See that ship?" Callum pointed.

"Yes," Charles nodded.

"That is the ship with your Uncle Hamish, Aunt Georgiana and your cousins."

Charles clapped his hands.

"I believe the cousins are the primary cause of excitement," Charlotte said.

"That's fine," Callum said. "We do only have one child."

Charlotte's eyes shimmered.

Why was she smiling at him in that manner?

Naturally, she was prone to smile. He didn't understand why people had thought her disagreeable. She could be precise in her words, but Callum found her most agreeable. He glanced at the way her long neck curved and the slender form of her hands.

Yes.

Charlotte was most agreeable.

In every sense.

"That's not entirely true," she said.

"What do you mean?" he asked.

"Only that Charles is not going to be the only child here."

"Because his cousins are coming."

Charlotte shook her head slightly. "I'd wanted to tell you before, but I wasn't certain."

"Heavens."

"Is it a good surprise?" Charlotte asked tentatively.

"It's the very best sort of surprise."

"They're here," Charles said gleefully and headed toward the dock.

Callum rushed after him happily, conscious the world was becoming fuller and more delightful than anything he could ever have anticipated.

Hamish sprang down the gangway, surrounded by his family and a slew of servants. Callum smiled. There'd been a time when his twin brother had lauded the virtues of privacy, but that was firmly in the past.

"How nice to see you," Callum said, realizing that he meant it.

Hamish beamed. "Aye."

They embraced and walked to the town. Warmth brushed over him.

Joyful shouts and bells sounded, and they looked over to the church.

"Someone is getting married," Charlotte murmured.

Thick brown doors opened, and a wedding couple stepped outside. Callum didn't know who these people were, but his heart still filled with joy at memories of his own wedding. Children flung petals at the couple, and everyone applauded. The woman's gown was not elaborate, but she wore a crown of flowers.

He squeezed Charlotte's hand, and her eyes sparkled.

"I do adore weddings," she said. "They always remind me of ours."

"I feel the same."

"But I adore our marriage more," she murmured, and he kissed her.

About the Author

BORN IN TEXAS, BIANCA Blythe spent four years in England. She worked in a fifteenth-century castle, though sadly that didn't actually involve spotting dukes and earls strutting about in Hessians.

She credits British weather for forcing her into a library, where she discovered her first Julia Quinn novel. Thank goodness for blustery downpours.

Bianca now lives in California with her husband.

Wedding Trouble

Don't Tie the Knot

The Earl's Christmas Consultant

How to Train a Viscount

A Kiss for the Marquess

A Holiday Proposal

MATCHMAKING FOR WALLFLOWERS

How to Capture a Duke

A Rogue to Avoid

Runaway Wallflower

Mad About the Baron

A Marquess for Convenience

The Wrong Heiress for Christmas

THE SLEUTHING STARLET

Murder at the Manor House

Danger on the Downs

The Body in Bloomsbury

A Continental Murder

Made in the USA
Middletown, DE
02 January 2021